"It seems we're both terrible at controlling ourselves, huh?"

Cassie shook her head and moved even closer to Brock. "I'm done controlling myself," she said.

Brock moved back just enough to look her straight in the eyes.

"I got some good advice today. If I wait until the boys are grown to do anything for myself, it might be too late, and I don't want that. It won't hurt them if I'm a little selfish and impulsive for the next nine days."

"Nine days," Brock repeated, though Cassie couldn't quite tell what emotion he was feeling when he said it.

She nodded resolutely, as much for herself as for him. "Until the rodeo. We can work on the house, and in the small snatches of time when the boys aren't around, we can do...more grown-up activities."

Brock smiled.

"We better make them a good nine days."

Dear Reader,

A new book is always an exciting and nerve-racking challenge, but starting a new book in a new series in an entirely new line takes it to a whole different level. Oh, and don't forget the rambunctious toddler who just *loves* to press buttons on my laptop!

Suffice it to say, writing this book taught me a lot about myself, and I'm thankful for all of the people who helped, especially my husband and my amazing editor, Johanna.

Despite the challenges, I can't wait to write more novels set in little Spring Valley, and I'm happy there are so many characters left whose stories need to be told. I look forward to writing them and giving each of them the happily-ever-after they deserve.

The McNeals—a family of adopted siblings, a meddling mother and a sweetheart father—have stolen my heart. I hope they do the same to you.

Happy reading,

Ali

THE BULL RIDER'S TWIN TROUBLE

Ali Olson

H HARLEQUIN® WESTERN ROMANCE

Recycling programs
for this product may
not exist in your area.

ISBN-13: 978-1-335-69953-4

The Bull Rider's Twin Trouble

Copyright © 2018 by Mary Olson

Printed in U.S.A.

Ali Olson is a longtime resident of Las Vegas, Nevada, where she has been teaching English at the high school and college levels for the past seven years. Ali has found a passion for writing sexy romance novels, both contemporary and historical, and is enthusiastic about her newly discovered career. She loves reading, writing and traveling with her husband and constant companion, Joe. She appreciates hearing from readers. Write to her at authoraliolson.com.

Books by Ali Olson

Harlequin Blaze

Her Sexy Vegas Cowboy
Her Sexy Texas Cowboy

Visit the Author Profile page
at Harlequin.com for more titles.

For my siblings.

To Claire, for her enthusiasm; to Alaina, for her love and support; and to Jerrod, because I think you'll be embarrassed having a romance novel dedicated to you and that amuses me.

Chapter One

Brock McNeal breathed deeply, moving his body in time with the jumping, twisting animal beneath him, and counted the seconds. *Six...seven...eight.*

The whistle sounded and he jumped off the bucking bull as bullfighters surrounded them, rolling to his feet and away from the large animal.

Brock soaked in the roar of the crowd. It hadn't been a great ride, he knew, but he'd hung on to Big Tex, one of the wildest bulls he had ever faced, and the audience was showing their appreciation. He tipped his hat to them and slid a wink over to a group of buckle bunnies holding signs, their skintight clothing leaving little to the imagination.

He almost didn't hear the shouts behind him as he basked in the glow of the crowd, but eventually he registered that something was wrong in the ring. Before he could turn around, two thousand pounds of animal flesh and muscle slammed into Brock, pushing him to the ground.

A hoof slammed into the ground inches from his face, kicking dirt into his eyes. Brock lay still, waiting for the next hoof, the one that would break his arm, puncture a lung or crack his skull.

After another few seconds, he opened his eyes to see the sky above him. The bullfighters had pulled the stomping, twisting bull away and out of the ring. The audience was silent, waiting to see how injured he was.

Brock jumped to his feet, tossed another smile to the people noisily showing their approval and walked out of the ring to join the other riders, enjoying the feeling of adrenaline pounding through his veins.

After receiving congratulations from the pack of men, Brock set off toward his truck.

"You trying to get yourself killed?" a gruff voice demanded the moment Brock was alone.

He turned to find his uncle standing behind him, hands on his hips. He looked angrier than Brock had seen him in a long while.

Brock gave him what he hoped was a calming smile. "I'm fine, Uncle Joe. Not a scratch," he said, raising his hands for inspection, or possibly in surrender to his uncle's fury.

"That was dangerous, and *stupid*, Brock. You know not to hang around in the ring like that, especially not with a bull like Big Tex in there with you," Joe said, shaking his head. "Jeannie must be rolling in her grave right now. And what would Sarah say if she knew you were putting yourself at risk like that? My sisters would never forgive me if something happened to you. I'd be hounded in this world and the next."

Brock winced at the verbal assault. His mother had been dead for twenty years, since he was just a little boy, but it still bothered him to hear his uncle talk about her like that. And Brock knew that if his uncle said anything to Sarah, his ma, the woman who had raised him since his parents died, she would worry herself sick.

Uncle Joe seemed to realize he'd been harsh, and his expression softened. "You're lucky you survived today, you know."

Brock nodded, not saying anything. His uncle had been one of the best bull riders in his day, and it was only through his coaching that Brock had managed to turn it into a career.

"I don't know why I put up with you and your recklessness," Uncle Joe groused.

Brock stayed silent. His uncle always said things like that when he was angry, and Brock had learned it was best not to respond. Joe would keep coaching Brock as long as Brock wanted to ride, so there was no point fighting with the old man.

Joe seemed to have grumbled himself out on the matter, and he changed topics, to Brock's relief. "You're headin' home tonight, right? Sarah's been on my case about you going for a visit."

Brock nodded. "Ma's been especially persistent lately, so I'll be there for two weeks, until the next rodeo. Amy, Jose and Diego will be coming into town in the next couple of days, too."

It had been a long while since Brock had seen his adopted brothers and sister, and he was sure Ma was in a tizzy waiting for her kids to come home. Sarah and her husband, Howard, had treated Brock like their own child since he was eight years old, and his adopted siblings even longer. Even though they were technically his aunt and uncle, he never thought of them as anything but his parents.

Joe nodded. "Keep your nose clean and I'll see you at the rodeo."

Brock couldn't help but smile. He was pretty sure it would be impossible to get into any trouble in a one-stoplight town like Spring Valley, Texas.

His uncle seemed to know what he was thinking, because he pointed his finger at Brock's chest. "Don't give me any guff, boy. I don't know how you manage to get yourself in the scrapes you do, smart as you are."

Brock considered saying that what Uncle Joe considered "scrapes" usually involved other men from the rodeo, whom he'd met through Joe himself, but he kept his mouth shut. If he wasn't careful, he'd be there all night listening to a lecture.

Brock tipped his hat in silent promise to keep his nose clean, then he turned back to the parking lot. "I better get on the road. I'll tell Ma you said hi."

The older man nodded. "Take care of yourself and don't do anything foolish," he said before heading back toward the large arena, from which sound erupted as another cowboy tried for his chance at the purse.

Brock turned toward his truck, the silver behemoth glinting in the afternoon sun, just one of many in the parking lot, waves of heat floating above the sea of metal. It was still early enough that most of the audience and competitors wouldn't be leaving for another hour or more.

Normally he would have stayed to talk to the other

cowboys, watch the last few rides, the closing ceremonies and possibly even the musical performance scheduled after the rodeo ended—and maybe get to know a few buckle bunnies while he was at it—then top the whole thing off with late-night drinks and planning the next big adventure with his friends. But he had a long drive ahead of him and he wanted to get to his parents' house before it was too late for a good meal, so he took one last look at the stadium behind him and opened the door to his truck, allowing the wave of pent-up heat to pass over him.

He wished he had his motorcycle with him so he could enjoy the sweeping curves of the mountain roads at top speeds, feel the rush of adrenaline and the wind at the same time. When he was on the circuit, though, it stayed in storage back in Dallas, so his truck would have to do. Anyway, if he rode up to Spring Valley on his bike, he'd get an earful from his ma, and he'd already had enough of that for one day.

He couldn't say he was happy about spending the weeks before his next rodeo in his tiny hometown, without much of a chance to prepare. He wanted to earn a spot at the NFR in Las Vegas, one of the toughest rodeos around, and Brock knew he couldn't take time off without hurting his chances.

But at least he was sure to get big servings of his ma's delicious country cooking, and he'd manage to find some way to keep himself sharp. Also, he could spend time helping Pop with the small riding school he ran on their property, though Brock knew that any insinuation that his dad was too old to do the work would earn him more than a stern talking-to.

Brock cranked the AC, steered out of the crowded parking lot and turned south toward Spring Valley.

As THE SUN disappeared behind the mountains surrounding the small town and ranches of Spring Valley, Brock turned off his truck's engine and stretched. The sprawling house in front of him looked cool and welcoming against the heat of the evening, and the unmistakable smell of horses and jasmine was so familiar that he would have known he was home even with his eyes closed. It was a smell that filled him with nostalgia and even a little longing. He'd always loved working on the ranch.

But that wasn't the life for him, he knew, though at times he wished it was. Rodeo life took a toll on a man, not just physically, but mentally. Moving from city to city, following the rodeo circuit, left Brock weary and glad for the short respite of a visit home, even if it made him itch for something more challenging, more dangerous, at the same time.

He saw the front door open and pulled the reins on his wayward thoughts as his ma came bustling out, her grin wide and her arms open. He climbed out of his truck and walked toward the woman who had cared for him so much of his life.

The frail-looking older woman pulled Brock into a hug so tight he could hardly breathe. He smiled at her. "You miss me?"

She swatted him on the shoulder. "Don't give me any

attitude, boy. You've been gone too long and you know it. I oughta give your uncle Joe a piece of my mind. At least you didn't ride in here on that infernal motorcycle of yours," she said, shaking her head.

Before he could even attempt to respond, she continued, "Come in now, dinner should be ready in a few minutes. I made Howie wait until you got here. I knew my boy would be hungry."

Brock let Ma's words of reprimand and love wash over him as he followed her into the warmth and glow of home, smiling at how familiar it all was. Everything was just as it should be on McNeal Ranch.

The smell of fried chicken attacked his senses as soon as he crossed the threshold and his stomach growled in response. "You were right. I'm starving," he said, veering toward the kitchen and the delectable smells.

Before he reached his destination, however, his ma blocked his entrance. "Don't you go rummaging around in there. You'll need to wait 'til I'm finished with everything and we sit down at the table like civilized folks."

He stopped and heaved a theatrical sigh, hoping she might relent, but it seemed clear she wouldn't be swayed by pity. After another look at the determined set of her jaw, he shrugged. "Okay, okay, I'll go grab my things," he said, turning to head back out to his truck.

"Actually, I have a job for you to do," she said in a seemingly casual voice that didn't fool him for a second. Brock wondered if he would finally hear why she had been so insistent about him coming for a visit.

He raised his eyebrows and waited. In that same

falsely casual tone, she said, "A sweet widow moved into the old Wilson place. Cassandra Stanford. She needs some help fixing up things around there. I told her my strong son would be happy to lend her a hand. You should go introduce yourself before we sit down to eat."

Brock was slightly disappointed. She just wanted him to do some work for an old widow? He had been expecting some bigger reason than that. His mother had been so pushy about him coming home, he'd half expected a mail-order bride to be waiting on the doorstep when he arrived. Maybe Ma had finally stopped trying to get her kids hitched and settled down, and was focusing her energy on helping her neighbor instead.

Brock doubted it, but for the time being, he was happy to be out of his ma's crosshairs. The last several times he'd been home, she had spent most of the time hinting about one girl or another from his high school, and she was always disappointed when he left for the circuit again without anything to show for her efforts.

Even if she had some plan for him during his stay, he was glad to see that she wasn't entirely consumed in her schemes. And it would be good for his ma to have a new friend nearby. Maybe they could knit together or something. Or, he shuddered to think, they could team up and become the town matchmakers.

He held in the smile that would lead to questions and another smack on the arm and gave Ma a kiss on her cheek. "Sure, I can help. I'll go introduce myself."

She grinned like the cat that ate the canary. "Don't rush yourself back. The chicken still has a ways to go."

Brock turned and headed back out the door he had walked through just a couple of minutes before, cutting through a paddock instead of heading out to the road. The Wilsons had been talking about moving for years, and he knew the place had fallen into disrepair as they got older. Why an old woman would want to take on the job was beyond him.

The walk was quick, and he hurried up the steps to the front porch of the neighboring home, noting the squeak of one of the steps and the white paint that was flaking off the house, showing the wood beneath.

There was plenty to do to make this place like new, if his first impression was any indication, but he knew it was a solid construction with good land. Part of him wished *he* had been the one to buy this property. Not that he had the money for this place. A middling rodeo cowboy didn't pull in enough for that kind of down payment. A National Finals cowboy might, though.

And it wasn't that likely he had even a chance of making it to Vegas if he spent the next two weeks painting and mending porch steps. He hoped the widow didn't expect him to be working there too often, or he'd be in a bit of a pickle. If Ma was so desperate to have him around, why would she give him a big job that might eat into all the time he had at home?

Brock brushed the question aside and turned his mind to the task at hand. He'd go through a short introduction and make his way back for his hot meal just as quickly as he could, then he'd make a plan as to how he should go about fixing up this place while leaving time to prepare for the next rodeo. He knocked.

After a few seconds, the door opened and any thought of food or rodeos disappeared. He stared, caught off-guard by the lovely woman who stood there, the warm glow of the lit room behind her enveloping her in almost a halo of light.

Her dark brown hair fell around her shoulders in a mass of curls, framing an open, sweet face and lips that promised more than just smiles for the guy lucky enough to get to kiss them. It was impossible to tell if her eyes were more brown or green, and he wanted to get near enough to get a better look. The blood in his veins moved faster just at the notion of being that close to her.

His ma's designs suddenly became clear: it wasn't the widow she had wanted him to meet, it was the beautiful lady standing before him. The widow's daughter, maybe?

He silently thanked his mother for her interfering ways as his eyes slid lower and took in more of the amazing view, noting how her jeans hugged her hips and the tied button-down shirt that accentuated her slim waist, giving just a peek of midriff. The top was unbuttoned low enough to give more than a suggestion of the breasts beneath.

Everything about her set him on fire. She was rather petite but didn't seem frail in the slightest despite her stature. She gave off an air of feistiness. Brock liked feisty.

Brock realized that he'd stood there without speaking for far too long, and brought his eyes back to hers. He suddenly felt a bit like an awkward teenager, not a grown man of nearly thirty. It took all his effort to arrange his face into a cool, confident smile. "Hello, ma'am," he said, putting on a slightly thicker drawl than usual. Ladies liked the Southern drawl. "I'm Brock Mc-Neal. My folks live just over the way. They said Mrs. Stanford was in need of some help fixin' up this place, and I thought it best to come introduce myself."

A plan was already formulating in Brock's mind. Make nice to the old lady, get in good with the beautiful mystery woman, then ask her for a date. Easy enough. His only problem was that two weeks in town suddenly didn't seem near enough time if he could spend it enjoying her company.

The woman standing before him smiled. "Nice to meet you. Call me Cassie. Your mother was so sweet to offer your help. I really don't know how I would manage all of the work by myself."

Brock's mind shifted gears quickly. The widow wasn't some old woman at all. Which meant that Cassie was here all on her own. But was she mourning a recently lost husband? She didn't seem to be. Would it be wrong to ask her out?

Before he could come to a conclusion, there were noises behind her and two young boys shot into the doorway behind Cassie, their identical faces peering at him from behind Cassie's legs.

"Zach, Carter, say hello to Mr. McNeal. He'll be helping us fix up the place a bit," Cassie said.

Brock tried his hardest to keep the disappointment off his face, but he wasn't sure he succeeded.

Of course she had kids. There had to be something

or his ma would've just come out and told him about her sneaky little plan. She knew well enough by now he didn't plan on having any children, and that meant no dating women with kids, either.

When the boys chirruped quiet hellos, he gave them a little wave before turning his attention back to their too-beautiful mother. "It was nice to meet you, but I better get back for dinner," he said.

Cassie seemed to sense his suddenly urgent need to leave; she nodded and said, "But I'll see you tomorrow and we can discuss the repairs?"

The almost desperate look in her eyes was too much. "Sure thing," he responded before turning away from the door, cursing his own bad luck.

Why did she have to be a mom?

Chapter Two

Cassie closed the door, trying not to show just how shaky she was feeling. She took in a large gulp of air, as if she hadn't breathed properly since first opening the door.

She put her hand to her chest, trying to calm the beating heart beneath. As soon as she did it, she realized her fingers were only touching bare skin and she groaned. She'd been unpacking boxes in the warm living room and had answered the door without realizing she was wearing a shirt that showed far more skin than she would have otherwise.

What must he have thought, to see her standing in the doorway showing off her stomach and chest like that?

Her mind went from zero to naughty in an instant, and it took all her effort to bring it back to being appropriately embarrassed.

"He's got big arms," Carter commented, oblivious to his mother's mental gymnastics.

Oh, she had noticed his arms. She had noticed every single inch of him, from the shaggy sun-kissed brown hair under a battered cowboy hat all the way to his scuffed boots. Her eyes had eaten him up like so much candy the moment she had seen him standing on her porch. But she wasn't planning on telling her four-year-old son that. "Hopefully he'll be strong enough to do things I can't do all on my own to get this ranch working," she said, trying to maintain her concentration on the tasks at hand.

"We'll help, too," Zach responded, a look of such sincerity on his young face that her heart—and eyes—welled up at the sight.

"I know you will," she answered, ruffling the boy's dark curls, trying to keep the worry out of her voice.

It had seemed like a great idea only a couple of months ago. Purchase a ranch, get out of the city and live the life she'd always wanted. It seemed so simple. But she hadn't expected everything to cost quite so much, and now here she was with a broken-down ranch that needed to make money, somehow, and she didn't have the faintest clue how to go about it.

She knew that once she got her small doctor's office going in the front room of the ranch house, she would be able to make ends meet, but finances would likely be tight for a while, and a running, profitable ranch would help give her a cushion. Instead, she was going to need to pour money into this place before she could hope to get much out of it.

Finding this ranch for sale when she so desperately wanted to leave Minneapolis had seemed like fate, and she'd jumped at the chance. Now, it seemed more like a crazy whim she'd acted on without thinking it through.

Mrs. McNeal's offer of a helpful son had been a gift

from heaven, and she knew she could never turn down the assistance, even if the man on the doorstep made her think nothing but the most sinful of thoughts.

Cassie pictured the way he had been standing there looking her over, and she felt short of breath again. She had tried to behave as professionally as she could, despite the inclination to kiss this complete stranger. She was no longer a whimsical young woman who could give in to an impulse of that sort, no matter how strong.

It was more difficult than she'd like to admit, though. She did *not* look forward to seeing the man again, and she needed to keep her distance when those urges pushed her to do some very inappropriate things. If she had any choice, she would tell the neighbors she didn't require any help, after all. But she did, so there was nothing for it.

Cassie turned her thoughts back to her two sons, who were playing amid the boxes piled around the living room. "Time for bed," she told them, and they hopped up, racing for the bathroom.

Zach won, shutting the door in Carter's face. While he waited his turn, he went over to his mother and pulled on her arm. "Can you tell us the story about the time Dad saved the baby birds?" he asked, looking up to her with his large green eyes.

Cassie's heart squeezed tight. The boys idolized their father and always wanted to hear stories about him. He had only been gone for six months, and she couldn't face tarnishing their perfect image of him, so she had kept telling them the good stories over and over, keeping the not-so-good ones to herself. To them, he was a kind-hearted police officer who had died in an unfortunate car crash. She wanted it to stay that way.

Zach and Carter were by far the biggest reason why she couldn't bring a man into her life. They weren't ready. Especially not for someone like this Mr. McNeal, who carried an air of recklessness about him.

If only that recklessness wasn't so damn enticing.

"YOUR NEW NEIGHBOR seems nice," Brock told his ma as he piled mashed potatoes onto his plate, trying to keep any hint of emotion out of his voice.

The old woman was terrible at hiding her exasperation. She had been so interested to hear what had happened that he was surprised she hadn't been hanging out a window with binoculars and some kind of long-distance microphone like in an old spy movie.

Well, it served her right to be on tenterhooks for a while, after that bit of meddling. Not that she shouldn't already know exactly how it went. She was well aware of his rule.

A bite of delicious fried chicken later, he felt he had tortured her enough.

"No kids, ma. You know that."

She gave an exaggerated sigh. "Brock, I can't understand what you have against children, particularly those two. They're sweet things. And being around them might do you, and them, some good. Howie, tell him," she said, swatting her husband on the arm.

The elderly man looked up from his food slowly, clearly unwilling to join the conversation. His gray mustache shifted from side to side as he chewed. After it was clear he was expected to make some sort of contribution, though, he nodded slightly. "Fine boys," he said.

Sarah looked triumphant, as if that settled everything.

Brock shrugged. "You know how I feel about raising kids. Between the rodeo circuit and the kind of life I live—"

His ma snorted, making her thoughts clear on *that* score. He plowed on, regardless.

"—I don't want the responsibility of children hanging over me every time I go rock climbing or hop on my motorcycle."

He didn't need to say any more. His adopted parents knew that he would never want to leave children without a father. When his parents had died…well, it wasn't something he would wish on anyone.

He turned his attention to his food, the air thick with unspoken words.

Still, if there was ever a woman who could make him consider breaking his "no kids" rule, it was this Cassie. Even then, the only type of relationship he was prepared to have with her would need to be something temporary, casual, especially when he'd be on the road again in another couple of weeks, and he doubted she would be okay with something like that. Not a widow with two young children.

It was best not to even start something, no matter how tempting the lady.

His ma shook her head at him. "Why you and your sister can't be happy with a nice calm life, I'll never know. With her always thousands of miles away and you doing reckless heaven-knows-what…at least your brothers don't try me like the two of you."

Brock bit his tongue, but he was sure Ma knew what he was thinking: what she called "reckless," he called fun, interesting, exciting.

"Where's Amy going after her visit?" he asked, hoping to change the subject.

"She said she needs to write an article about Morocco or something," Ma said, still glowering. "It's as if you two have a bet going to see who can make the last of my hairs gray the fastest."

Brock had to laugh at that. He'd never told Ma about the time the previous winter that he'd nearly snowboarded off a cliff face when a storm blew up around him, or a dozen other adventures he'd had in the last few years, but he could imagine her hair going pure white if she ever found out about it. He wondered if Amy had been keeping similar secrets from their ma.

The older woman harrumphed, but didn't say anything more on the subject, and for that he was grateful. They'd had the "When are you going to settle down?" conversation so many times that another run-through just sounded exhausting.

After eating, Brock climbed the stairs to his childhood room, too tired from the competition earlier in the day and the long ride home to think about much of anything. Before he went to sleep, however, the image of Cassie floated before his eyes, and he drifted off with a smile on his lips.

THE NEXT MORNING dawned hot and still, the sky quickly turning from soft lavender to a bright, cloudless blue. Cassie was awake but kept her eyes shut, not wanting to let go of the luxurious feeling that had come with whatever dream she had been having. Most of it had slipped away the moment she awoke, but she remembered one part of it with a vivid clarity: strong arms encircling her, holding her close to a warm muscular body.

She sighed and opened her bleary eyes, pulling herself off her bed, which was currently nothing more than a mattress and box spring on the floor. The time for dreaming was over, and that dream in particular had no place in her very busy day. She looked around the bedroom full of cartons, her eyes passing from the unfinished Ikea dresser to the headboard leaning against one wall, waiting to be attached to a bed frame she hadn't gotten around to putting together. She sighed again and started rummaging in one of the boxes for something to wear.

They had moved into the house two weeks before, but with the delays from the moving company and two raucous boys with no friends in town yet, she had hardly made a dent in the mounds of containers everywhere. Most of her time had simply been spent assessing what needed to be fixed and trying to organize the mass of paperwork the Wilsons left her about the property, none of which helped much.

What had she been thinking, buying this place and moving them all out here to chase some childish dream of hers? The thought had flitted through her mind over and over again since they'd arrived.

Without noticing, she had gotten to the bottom of the box of clothes, and her hand touched something silky. Curious, she pulled out whatever it was she'd found, promptly dropping it in surprise. The lingerie fell to the floor, a small pool of black silk and lace.

She didn't remember packing it, had even forgotten she'd ever purchased the thing. It was years ago now, when she was trying to keep her marriage afloat. It was a reminder that she had once hoped to have an exciting love life, the sort of thing she was now avoiding.

Cassie shook her head slightly and shoved the thing into the bottom of the box marked "Pajamas," then went back to picking something practical to wear. She pulled on jeans and a blouse, trying to forget the sexy black teddy, only to have the concerns about her new ranch rush back in on her.

She tried to make those thoughts go away, too. It was too late to second-guess her decision to put an offer on the ranch and sign the mortgage paperwork, so she might as well stop it and just look ahead to what needed to get done so their new home would run smoothly. Now that she'd have someone helping who might know a thing or two about how to do that, she felt hopeful about the progress that would be made.

If she could manage to keep her hands off him, of course.

She walked out of her depressingly cluttered room without looking at it again. That would need to wait until she dealt with more pressing matters, like when she could start seeing patients and figuring out how she could get the ranch to make money.

She let the worry drift to the back of her mind as she entered the living room, where Zach and Carter were using the piles of boxes and some blankets to make a fort. She smiled and crawled through the little doorway they had created using two kitchen chairs and a rug. Before she spent the day trying to be a doctor and a rancher, she could spend an hour being a mom to her two boys. That, at least, wasn't overwhelming.

They weren't very far along on their fort, however, when there was a knock on the door that made her heart sink. There was only one person who could be on the other side of that door, and despite how much she needed his help, she wasn't looking forward to seeing the handsome Mr. McNeal again, especially not after her dream from the night before. Zach jumped up, his head grazing the blanket that made the fort roof. "I'll get it!" he shouted, diving between the two chairs.

She listened to his quick footsteps and the squeak of the front door. When she heard the deep rumble of Brock McNeal's voice as he spoke to Zach, her face flushed. She steeled herself for a long day of pretending not to notice how attracted she was to him.

And how attracted he is to you, a little voice inside her added. Her mind drifted back to what hid in the bottom of her box of pajamas. She quelled all that immediately. Sure, she'd seen the way he had looked her over when she'd opened the door the previous night, but she had also seen the way his face fell when Zach and Carter joined her. She knew what that look meant, and it was enough to make her even more sure that she would keep her distance from this man.

If he wasn't interested in a woman with kids, well, it just made things that much easier. She took a deep breath, glanced down to make sure her shirt was more modest than yesterday and began trying to extricate herself from the tiny fort.

BROCK FOLLOWED THE young boy into the home formerly owned by his old neighbors, Mr. and Mrs. Wilson, where he had played dozens of times as a kid. The house had a slightly dilapidated look about it, as if nobody had taken the time to keep it in good working order, but it was still clean and homey, the wallpaper and fixtures exactly as they had been twenty years before, and likely twenty years before that.

Though it was outdated and a little the worse for wear, it was of solid construction, a good home. He imagined there wouldn't be too much to do to get it up to snuff; hopefully the land was in a similar state and not too far gone to seed.

In the living room, the lovely woman of the evening before was crawling out of what was clearly a makeshift fort, her curly hair a messy tangle that hid half her face, her splendidly curved butt shown off in lovely detail.

How did she manage to make climbing out of a blanket fort sexy?

If he'd been out of sight, he would have smacked himself in the forehead to dislodge these wayward thoughts. It was clear to him that he'd need to help her as quickly as possible, and then keep his distance from this woman from then on out. If she got his heart pumping doing something so innocent, he needed to do everything in his power to protect himself.

She straightened up, looking even more deliciously tousled, and nodded to him with a small smile. "Thank you for coming, Mr. McNeal. I wasn't expecting you this early. I was just going to make some pancakes for the boys. Would you like some?"

Brock knew he should take the chance to get working while she was busy elsewhere, to ensure that he could concentrate on the manual labor without her nearby, but the thought of missing out on pancakes was disheartening. His ma was happy to make eggs and bacon but had never been one for pancakes—too sweet for a good start to the day, she'd always said. He forced himself to shake his head. "No, thanks, I already ate. I'll just get started on whatever you need me to do, if you don't mind."

Her mouth thinned a little and her cheeks blushed a light shade of pink. He realized that she really hadn't expected him yet, and she wasn't sure where he should start. She seemed to be at a loss for a moment.

Not that it was surprising she hadn't anticipated his early arrival. He'd woken at dawn, itching to get over there—to get started on all the work that needed to be done, he'd told himself. After all, two weeks wasn't much time, and he didn't want to leave his new neighbor in the lurch after he'd gone. So he'd headed over right after eating, without noticing exactly how early it was.

Brock decided that just because there was so much to do didn't mean there wasn't time for pancakes. "Actually, pancakes sound great. After all, there's probably enough work around here to burn off four breakfasts, I'm sure. And while you're at it, I'll take a look around to see what all there is to do, if that's all right?"

She nodded, looking relieved, and he immediately felt like he'd made the right choice. Plus, he would get to eat pancakes. That was a win-win.

"I'll go get them started. Please make yourself at home, Mr. McNeal."

"Call me Brock," he answered before she disappeared into the kitchen.

The moment she was gone, he looked around the room and started creating an inventory of everything that would need to be done to get the house in shape. Besides two warped window frames and the very faded wallpaper, the living room at least appeared in decent condition.

"Would you like to come in our fort?" one of the boys asked suddenly, poking his head out between two boxes.

Brock had forgotten he wasn't alone in the room. He gave the kid a small smile. "No, thanks," he said, not sure if there was anything else he was supposed to say.

It had been a long while since he'd spoken to anyone under the legal drinking age.

The other boy, identical to his brother, crawled out of the fort and moved to stand right next to Brock. Brock waited, wondering what the little boy was thinking. Finally, he spoke. "I'm Carter."

Brock nodded, wishing the child wasn't quite so close. He wasn't used to children and their lack of understanding about personal space. "Hi. I'm Brock," he answered.

Carter kept staring, as if waiting for Brock to say more, but he couldn't think of what else he should say.

"What are you doing?" the boy asked.

"I'm trying to figure out what we need to do to get this place fixed up," Brock answered.

Carter looked around the room. "Like what?"

Brock felt slightly relieved that the large hazel eyes were no longer staring at him in that intense way. He pointed out the windows, explaining about the frames.

"Momma tried to open those when we got here and couldn't," Carter commented. "What else is wrong?"

Brock shrugged. "I don't know. I just got here."

With that, Carter was off, pointing out every problem he had noticed since they'd moved there. Some, like the faint scratches on the wood floor from furniture being moved around, didn't concern Brock, but there were others that he added to the mental list he was making.

Soon, Brock and Carter had moved into the room the boys were sharing and Brock was examining the large wooden bunk bed the boys would use once, as Carter explained, it didn't wobble anymore. "Momma says the Wilson boys must have been pretty rowdy to break such a big piece of furniture," Carter said as Brock pulled on the top bunk and watched it sway precariously. Brock smiled, remembering exactly how "rowdy" the Wilson boys were. They had gotten Brock into quite a bit of trouble more than once when he was a kid.

Carter continued talking, as if he had no plans to

stop anytime soon. "But it was free, so she said she would fix it and then we won't have to sleep on the floor no more."

"Anymore," said a voice from the doorway. The other brother, Zach, had joined them.

Brock nodded to him, then turned back to Carter. "It'll be easy to fix. A couple planks of wood and some nails will do it."

"There's some in the barn. Momma showed me."

Brock stood, ready to go find them, but Zach interrupted his thoughts. "Mom says food's ready, Mr. McNeal."

Before Brock could say anything, Carter jumped up and grabbed his hand. "We have to wash up before we eat. I'll show you." And with that, Brock was being pulled into a small bathroom and shown how to clean his hands properly.

Brock washed at the sink and followed Carter and Zach into the kitchen, where the boys jumped into chairs, both sitting on their feet so they could see over the table. The moment he was back in the same room as Cassie, the air felt warm and heavy, neither of which had anything to do with the cooking.

Brock tried not to let his eyes wander along the length of her legs as she stood by the stove, flipping the last pancakes on the griddle. The jeans she was wearing hugged her in all the right places, and a long study of them would just make things worse.

He was here to do a job, help a lady and her kids out, and then he would get back to doing the things he did best. After all, his next big bull ride was coming up soon. It wouldn't do to start getting sidetracked by a mess of russet-colored hair and a pair of shapely legs. Or any of her other attributes he had noticed.

With difficulty, Brock pulled his eyes to the plate in the middle of the table piled high with flapjacks. The smell wafting from them was light and sweet, and they made his mouth water despite the large breakfast he'd already had. The boys had quickly grabbed a couple and begun dousing them in syrup, so he speared a few of his own with his fork.

Cassie came to the table, taking the only open seat, the one directly across from him. Now that she was close and in the bright light of the kitchen, he could see a dusting of freckles across her nose and the clear green-brown of her eyes. When she leaned forward to grab her own pile of pancakes, he quickly glanced away. There was too much to catch all of his male attention when she did that.

Thankfully, she soon sat back in her seat and he could actually savor the flavor of the pancakes he had shoved into his mouth in a desperate bid for a distraction.

She didn't seem to notice any of this and her attention remained focused on her children. "Did you both wash up before coming in and getting covered in syrup?" she asked.

Carter nodded as he licked some of the sticky sweetness off his forearm. "I showed Brock how to wash up, too," he said.

Cassie gave her son a warning look. "Don't be impolite. You can call him Mr. McNeal."

"It's fine," Brock cut in, not wanting Carter to get in trouble for his actions. "I told him he could call me that. I think the only person who has ever called me Mr. McNeal was my fourth-grade teacher, and that lady was plumb crazy."

Carter smiled at him. Brock couldn't help but smile back.

Cassie also seemed pleased, though she wasn't as obvious in her emotions as Carter was. "Well, now that that's settled," she said, "I was thinking we would start working in the library first, and then some of the fencing around the place, or maybe the barn. I want to get the ranch ready to hold horses."

He nodded, trying to keep his eyes on his plate instead of on her. Hopefully she would show him where to start and leave him to it, and he could lose himself in hard work and avoid this woman who set his blood on fire.

After she dumped the dishes in the sink, though, she looked at her two boys and said, "While we're moving things around, I'd like you to put your clothes into the drawers in your room. After that, you can work on your fort or play with your cars. Can you do that?"

So, she clearly wasn't planning on freeing him from her presence. If he hadn't been pleased that she was willing to get her hands dirty and help fix up the place, he would've been annoyed about spending even more time near her.

The boys nodded and raced into their room. Brock was impressed that such young children could follow directions, but before he could comment, Cassie smiled at him and shook her head. "They'll probably throw everything in one drawer before getting sidetracked and playing with toys, but it'll keep them busy for a few minutes, at least."

Brock pictured himself doing just that as a kid and laughed. Her dry humor only made her prettier, which sobered him quickly. "So, you wanted to start in the Wilsons' old library?" he prompted.

Cassie nodded and walked out of the kitchen, beckoning at Brock to follow her. He took a deep breath and tried to ignore the well-formed bottom that swayed so enticingly before him.

Chapter Three

Cassie showed Brock into the small room off the living room that she hoped to turn into a doctor's office. Before she could start seeing patients, however, there was a lot to do.

The room had obviously been used as a library. The empty shelves lining the wall were of dark oak, making the entire space feel shady and somber. She imagined leather chairs and dusty volumes of old books giving it an air of class, but it didn't fit with the light, friendly tone she wanted to convey.

"Mr. Wilson was quite a reader," Brock commented, looking around the room. "I never understood why they lived on this ranch when he would have been much happier being a professor or something. What do you want to do with it?"

"I want to take out these shelves and make it into a doctor's office," she started, ready to turn her dream into a reality.

"You're a doctor?" he asked, clearly surprised.

She nodded, waiting to see how he would react. Her husband, Hank, had always been negative about her choice to continue school instead of staying home with their young children, and even though he'd been gone for over six months, she still heard his disapproving words in her ears.

Brock gave her a sideways grin that turned her insides to mush. "You're full of surprises," he commented, and she couldn't stop the blush of pleasure that worked its way up to her ears. "Well, the town certainly needs a doctor. People are going to line up at your door. So I guess we should get this place ready."

Then he turned back to the room as if nothing had changed. Cassie's defenses lowered slightly as she accustomed herself to Brock's presence.

"Okay, so the shelves need to go," he said. "What do you need to make the room ready?"

With that, she was off, describing the room she had imagined. A small desk, some shelves to hold supplies, bright paint, a couple of chairs and an examination table. A happy place where she could help people.

Brock listened, nodding occasionally. When she finished, he stretched, his arms raised to the ceiling. Cassie tried not to stare at him, but it wasn't easy. "Let's get started, then," he said, moving farther into the room.

Soon they were grappling with the bookcases—heavy bulky things that, thankfully, took all her attention. With some difficulty, they managed to get the three large shelving units on their sides and slide each one out the door until they were lying in a row on the living room floor.

With those out, the room seemed much larger and brighter, and Cassie's heart lifted. She knew she could make it into everything she wanted. Then she realized there was one big problem that prevented her from doing more.

Brock seemed to sense her sudden change of mood. "You don't have paint yet, do you?"

Cassie shook her head, trying not to feel too disappointed.

"Then we'll need to get some. We can do that tomorrow morning, if you like. For now, on to the next thing," Brock announced, sidling out of the room.

Cassie could tell he wasn't going to let her sulk, and it made her smile. He was right, anyhow. There was too much to do to sit around just because she didn't have paint.

Back in the living room, they both looked at the shelves taking up most of the floor space. "I guess we could put two of these in my room and the other in Zach and Carter's," she said at last.

Brock moved into place to pick up one of the units and waited for her. Cassie couldn't believe how willing he was to haul them all over her house, without a word of protest. She silently thanked Brock's mother for having such a helpful son.

Soon all her thoughts and energy were once again absorbed by the task of lifting the heavy pieces of furniture, which they lugged down the hall.

Maneuvering the first one into her bedroom was a bit of a challenge, but finally the shelf stood against the wall opposite her bed. If the room wasn't large, it might have looked hefty, but Cassie felt it fit nicely. She turned to Brock to see if he was ready to move the second one, and found him standing awkwardly near the doorway.

Then she realized that they were in her bedroom and she felt a flush creep up her neck at the memory of what lay at the bottom of her box of pajamas, only a couple of feet from where she was standing.

Brock cleared his throat and looked at her, but didn't quite meet her eyes, for which she was thankful. Now was not the time to get lost in those ocean-colored depths. "Let's go grab the next one," he said, leaving for the hallway.

Cassie followed, hoping the heat in her cheeks would go away before they looked at each other again.

BROCK WAS GLAD to return to the open air of the living room. Even though the master bedroom in the Wilson house was large, the presence of Cassie and her bed made him feel short of breath and a little claustrophobic.

But that wasn't the way his thoughts should be turning, he knew.

They made quick work of the second shelf, and without pausing in Cassie's room, for which Brock was grateful, moved onto the third. As Brock picked up his end, he could feel the strain in his back, a holdover from an old rodeo injury. If he was tired, he imagined Cassie must be exhausted. He almost set down the shelf again to propose they take a break, but before he could, Cassie had lifted her end and begun moving toward the hallway with dogged determination on her face.

Brock couldn't help but be impressed. She didn't shirk the work it was going to take to get this place running, that was for sure. They carried the thing into the boys' room, where they set it up against the wall as the two boys watched from where they'd been playing on the floor. When it was in place, Cassie leaned against it to catch her breath. Brock took the chance to stretch his back.

"Did you boys finish putting all your clothes away before playing?" Cassie asked after a few moments.

The children nodded, but Brock noticed they seemed a little hesitant. He glanced over at the chest of drawers. From the look of the bursting bottom drawer, Cassie's earlier prediction seemed to have come true. She noticed, too, and she opened it wider. "I don't think you'll be able to find anything in here," she told them, with an impressive amount of patience. "How about we work on this together?"

Brock could see this might take a while, so he left Cassie with her kids and went back to the library. This woman just kept getting more and more attractive. A beautiful, hardworking doctor with the patience of a saint. He shook his head in amazement.

He wanted to ask her out. What harm could a date do? He imagined she could use an evening being pampered.

There was one big flaw with that idea, though: What if she said no? He didn't want the next couple of weeks to be awkward as they worked on her house and ranch together. Or worse, she felt so uncomfortable that she insisted on doing it all by herself, even though it was clearly too big a job for just one person.

So he wouldn't ask her out yet, then. Not until he was sure she'd say yes, or until enough work was finished that he wouldn't feel guilty if he got turned down and was asked to never see her again.

He hoped to God that wouldn't happen.

What about her kids? A small voice inside him piped up.

Well, it would just be a date. Nothing serious. He wasn't going to turn everything in his life upside down because of a passing attraction. They'd go on a few dates, have a nice time and then he'd leave. If they both agreed to nothing permanent, neither of them could get hurt, right?

Brock felt a twinge of uncertainty but dismissed it. If he had to choose between a temporary relationship with Cassie or no relationship at all, he knew which side he fell on. The thought lifted his spirits, and he looked around eagerly for something to accomplish.

Near the library, leaning against a wall, were some boxes with pictures of small white shelves on them. They were clearly pieces of furniture for her future doctor's office, and would need to be assembled before she could start seeing patients.

He immediately set to work on the first one.

The task went quickly, and by the time Cassie appeared, he was halfway through the second, with instructions and pieces surrounding where he sat on the floor. Seeing her made his heart beat harder, and he found it difficult to remember what it was he'd been doing. She caressed the top of the completed piece in such a way that it took every bit of his self-control to not ask her out right then and there.

"Thank you for your help," she said, so sincerely

that it squeezed at his heart. It was clear from her tone that she'd desperately needed an extra pair of hands.

"I imagine it's hard to get much done with two young boys around," he commented.

She let out a sigh of agreement and nodded. "They're putting things on their new shelf now, so that should give them something to do for a little while, at least," she said, sitting down beside him and leaning close to look at the instructions.

For a moment, she was too close, and he wanted more than ever to do something about the feelings crowding in him. As he opened his mouth to say something stupid, she moved away again, and his mind cleared enough to keep quiet. She didn't seem to notice, and before he could get out of his daze enough to get back to the task at hand, she was grabbing pieces and fitting them together with nimble, quick movements.

With some effort, Brock turned back to his own work, and they flew through the rest of the low-lying shelves, two cabinets and several small drawers. He imagined them holding cotton swabs, latex gloves and myriad other items that a doctor would need in order to care for the people who came to her. From the way Cassie was smiling as she touched each completed piece, she could, too.

When they were finished with the last drawer, Cassie sat back and looked around her at all they'd done. Brock could only stare at her. She was endlessly fascinating. They had worked almost entirely without speaking, anticipating each other's motions in a way he couldn't describe. They had been assembling a few inexpensive pieces of furniture, but it had felt more like a dance where they moved in harmony together.

He stood and started placing the completed items against the wall, out of the way until they could be placed into the new office. The silence that had been comfortable a few minutes before became thick, and he grasped for something to talk about. "What's the next big task on your to-do list?" he said, hoping she didn't notice the strained sound of his voice.

"Until I have paint, we've done about as much on the office as we can. I guess the next big part—"

He hoped she wouldn't say her bedroom. He'd noticed the boxes and incomplete bedframe, but boy howdy, an hour in her bedroom seemed much more dangerous than jumping out of an airplane or climbing on the back of a bull right now.

"—would be the fence, or maybe the barn," she finished.

Brock exhaled with relief.

"Well," he started, considering the best plan of action, "we should probably take a walk along the perimeter, see where the fence needs to be fixed or replaced."

Brock wasn't sure if he really thought the entire fence needed to be checked or if he was just torturing himself with a long, private stroll with Cassie. He didn't need to worry about the latter, though, because Cassie immediately stood and said, "I'll go get Zach and Carter. They'll be happy to get out of the house," before disappearing down the hall toward the boys' room.

CASSIE WAS GLAD FOR the twins' company as they all walked out into the late-morning sun. The hours she had spent with Brock already that day made her very aware that she needed chaperones, if only to keep herself from doing something stupid like kissing him.

Luckily, her children were excellent distractions.

As soon as they were out of the house, the boys were tearing around like two tiny dust storms, creating havoc wherever they went and only stopping occasionally to ask Brock questions about life as a cowboy.

Through his answers, she learned that he was visiting his parents for two weeks and that he worked on the circuit—though she wasn't entirely sure what that meant. The boys were thrilled to discover that he owned a truck *and* a motorcycle. And that he liked horses and owned lots of cowboy hats and boots.

From the way he answered each question without a sign of irritation, she also realized that Brock was patient, good-natured and kind. She wished he was just a little bit worse of a human being, so she'd have something to grasp to that might help her get over her overwhelming attraction to him.

Finally, she cut into the questions, both because she wanted to save Brock from the unending list the boys seemed to have, and because she was curious what he was doing as he examined a fence post.

"Boys, why don't you race each other to that tree?" she suggested, pointing out a small oak a hundred yards or so in the distance. Zach and Carter ran off, their excess energy seeming to burst out of every seam.

Cassie turned to Brock. "What are you checking

for?" she asked, wondering if she sounded like the young boys.

"To see if the wood is rotten or not. If you have rot, you'll need to replace those sections, or they might come down not long from now. It'll be a lot of extra work, though."

"And money, I'm sure," Cassie said, biting her lip.

She would need to get her doctor's office going, and soon, or at this rate she and the boys would be living off peanut butter sandwiches for the foreseeable future.

Brock nodded. "But the fence can wait, if you aren't planning on keeping animals out here, in which case we could just fix the paddock and barn."

Cassie gazed across the land covered in tall grass the color of gold. What would she do with the crops? She had just wanted a ranch with some horses, but it was becoming more and more obvious that she didn't know the first thing about ranching...

Maybe her mother was right: she was getting in way over her head. She was just a city girl playing rancher, and she didn't know the game.

"Everything okay?" Brock asked, pulling her out of her reverie.

She started to nod but couldn't bring herself to pretend. "There's just so much I need to figure out," she answered, looking at him.

The sympathy in his dark blue eyes made her heart thump heavily, and she had difficulty keeping control of herself.

He looked out over her ranch and she took the chance to catch her breath. After a few moments, he nodded.

"It'll be a lot of work, but it's a good piece of land. Do you have a buyer for the hay you won't use?"

She shook her head, feeling stupid. She didn't even have any idea how to turn the grass waving in front of her into hay bales, let alone what to do with it. "I don't—"

Cassie stopped talking, her voice catching in her throat. She had been told that the farm was growing grass to turn into hay, but she hadn't thought about what to do with it until she'd actually gotten here and seen it.

The enormity of the tasks before her threatened to overwhelm her. She could only imagine what Brock must think about her, purchasing this whole place without knowing how to do a single thing.

"This is my lucky day," Brock replied.

Cassie looked at Brock, surprised at the enthusiasm in his voice. Was he being sarcastic?

Brock hitched his thumb back toward his parents' ranch. "Pop could use a good chunk for their horses, and my brothers would be happy to buy the rest, I'm sure. And they'll pay to get the baling machine out here, too, if you don't already have one lined up. It's my lucky day because this means almost my entire family will owe me, which can be useful in the McNeal house."

Cassie laughed, more out of astonishment than anything. "Do you really think your brothers would do all that?" she asked, trying not to get her hopes up too high, but unable to suppress the grin that came to her lips.

Brock nodded, smiling back. "They just started a

business working with rodeo stock, and I'm sure they could use it. They'll give you a fair price."

A weight lifted off Cassie, and she felt some of the tension in her shoulders ease. She would be able to sell the hay. If she could do that, start seeing patients, mend the fence and make the barn livable for her horses, maybe everything would be all right. It was a big if, but it was something.

"You'll want to keep a bit of it for your own horses, right? I know the Wilsons had a couple."

She nodded, picturing Rosalind and Diamond, the two mares that had come with the property. "If I can get the barn and fencing in shape enough to keep them here, yes. For now, they're being kept at a place a few miles away."

"Well, we can figure out what lumber you need for the fence and paddock, but mend the paddock first. That way, you can move the horses here sooner. They don't need a perfect barn in this weather, so those little fixes can wait."

She didn't say anything about the boarding costs, yet another worry on her plate. Cassie suddenly felt embarrassed, as if every shortcoming and difficulty of hers was being laid bare in front of this man she'd known less than twenty-four hours.

Despite how much she appreciated his help, she also felt slightly uncomfortable with how much she needed it. She'd always been self-sufficient, smart and able to do whatever she put her mind to. This whole thing wasn't great for her ego, that was for sure.

Still, she'd gotten herself into this mess, and right

now she just needed to worry about surviving it with as much of her dignity intact as she could manage. As long as nothing else landed on her plate, she would be able to handle it.

She hoped.

Chapter Four

Brock looked at Cassie, his heart going out to her. He could tell she was anxious, with her lips pinched so tightly together. It seemed like a world of worries was swirling about in her head.

"So, with the hay issue settled and our next job planned, we can get back to checking the fence," he said, hoping to get her attention on the here and now, and away from her thoughts. "With the perimeter fence, if you're only growing crops, we can just repair it a bit, but if you plan to have any animals roaming around, we'll need to make sure it's perfectly solid. Do you think you'll have stock out here, or just crops?"

Apparently his question didn't help at all, because she only looked more worried, and he could see that tears were threatening to fall. Even though they had only met the day before, he couldn't stand by and watch without doing something. As if on the same impulse, he pulled her into a hug as she threw herself against him. "I don't know what I'm doing here," she said, her voice muffled against his chest.

"Momma? You okay?" Carter asked.

Brock looked down, startled to see the boys. They

had finished the race apparently, and were standing side by side with expressions of concern on their identical faces.

Cassie broke away from his chest and smiled down at her children. "I'm fine, honey. I was giving Mr. McNeal a hug. Because he's being so nice to help us."

Brock stood there, not sure what to say. The moment had been so raw, so pained, and yet she was able to put it all aside for her little boys. He had to wonder if she'd done the same thing when her husband died, burying her hurt in order to stay strong for her children. He was almost sure she had.

He was truly amazed by this woman.

"Let's keep walking," Brock said at last, trying to bring himself out of his own thoughts. "I'll check for rot, and we can figure it all out once we know what we're looking at. How does that sound?"

Cassie flashed him a grateful look, and they all continued along the perimeter of the land.

The boys immediately filled the silence with their questions and whatever else seemed to pop into their heads. Brock couldn't help but like them. His ma was right: they were sweet kids.

Zach grabbed Cassie's arm. "Momma! Tell about Daddy!"

Brock was glad he was already looking at a fence post and the lumber nailed to it—it gave him a chance to hide his reactions. Curiosity mixed with a little embarrassment, and maybe even some jealousy. The man had, after all, been married to Cassie, been father to these two boys. He couldn't help wanting to stack himself up against him, even if his good sense told him it was a bad idea in more ways than one.

Once he'd mastered his expression, Brock turned back to Cassie and the boys, hoping he seemed nonchalant. He was surprised to see the slight flush of red in Cassie's cheeks, and wondered if his presence was causing her to feel uncomfortable.

He moved ahead of the other three, just in case the distance might make her feel better. He couldn't help listening, though.

"Your daddy," she began, in a tone that made Brock sure she'd said these same words many times, "was one of the hardest workers in our precinct. He worked lots of hours trying to keep the city safe for everyone."

"He was a good policeman," Carter added, as if he held that knowledge close to his heart.

Brock felt heartbroken for these two boys, who had lost their father at such a young age. It brought back his own painful memories.

He didn't look at Cassie, kept his eyes on the fence, but he imagined her nodding and smiling at her son, remembering her brave police officer husband. Asking her out suddenly seemed like little more than a pipe dream.

"One time, he was driving along in his squad car," Cassie went on, "and he saw a man yelling at a woman, who was crying."

"That man was mean!" Zach shouted, angry.

"He was mean," Cassie agreed. "Your daddy went up and helped the woman, and the man couldn't hurt her anymore because your daddy was there to protect her. It's good to help and protect people who need it," she concluded.

The boys gabbled happily about the story, running on ahead. Brock stood with Cassie, unsure what to say. Complimenting her deceased husband didn't seem right, but neither did asking questions or completely ignoring what just happened.

Before he could figure out what to say, Cassie spoke to him, her voice quiet enough to keep the boys from overhearing. "Sorry. About before."

With the image of her husband looming large over Brock, he had almost forgotten her tears from just a few minutes ago.

He waved away the apology. "None of us know what we're doing all the time," he said.

She made a noise that could have been a snort, or perhaps a small sob. "It's not just a small case of indecision. I made all these choices, moving us all the way out here, without really thinking things through. I was so desperate to get away from—well, it doesn't matter. So I followed a silly childhood dream, and now the reality of it all is a bit much. My mom was right," she said with a small, sad laugh, "I was being too impulsive, too stubborn."

Brock smiled. "My ma says that about me all the time, too."

"Is she right?" Cassie asked, her voice quiet.

Brock could see she was hoping for something to hold on to. He shrugged. "Yeah, but I've got to make choices for myself, right? You can't be happy living the way other people want you to."

He watched her absorb his words. Finally, she nodded, wiping away a stray tear, and turned to the fence. "Is much of it decayed?" she asked.

He half wanted to bring the subject back to why she had come here, what she was running away from, but decided to let it lie. It probably had to do with her husband's death, and if she moved here because the memory of her lost love was too painful, he'd rather not know. Brock knocked on the fence board in front of him. "It seems like most of it is okay. It just needs some new nails and a fresh coat of paint. You'll need a few hundred bucks' worth of lumber, at most, if the rest of it is like this," he said, gesturing at the expanse of fence behind them.

Cassie seemed relieved, and they continued walking in silence. After a short while, Brock said, "You might want to consider raising a small herd of cows out here. It would cost a bit at first, but you can buy them as you can afford them, and they'll be more lucrative than selling bales of hay in the long run."

Brock wasn't sure if the information was helpful or more to add to her plate, but he felt sure, despite how little he knew about her, that she would appreciate knowing his opinion on the subject.

Cassie smiled. "Owning cows to go along with my horses, huh? That would make me a real country girl," she said, hooking her thumbs in her jean pockets.

He laughed. "Get some boots instead of those sneakers and a good hat, and nobody will know you're a city slicker."

She nodded, raising her hand to shade her face from

the sun's powerful rays. "I'll definitely need a hat, if it's always this sunny. I'm not used to the weather here."

"Where are you from?" he asked without thinking.

It was only after he said it that he remembered her earlier words. Wherever she was from, she had run to the country to get away from it. Brock felt like an ass for bringing it up, but it was too late now.

"Minneapolis," she said, without elaborating further.

Still, she didn't seem devastated by the question, and he was curious about her. *In for a penny, in for a pound*, he thought. "That's a pretty big city," he commented.

"Smaller than you might think," she answered in a light tone, but the expression on her face hardened slightly.

Something within him pushed to keep the conversation going as they continued along the fence. They were over halfway done, and he felt like this was an opportunity to get to know her. Something about the wide-open land and sky around them made it easier. "I can see why you haven't had much experience with land and fences up there. It's not exactly a ranching area. The winters are brutal there, aren't they?"

She rolled her eyes, and his heart jumped when she gave him a genuine smile. "Like you wouldn't believe. That's one of the reasons I picked Spring Valley. I'll be just fine if I never see snow again."

He wanted to keep her smiling. "Well, this is the place to be if you hate snow. It's a rare winter that we get more than an inch or two."

She nodded and looked fondly across the hot brown grass. Before the silence could stretch too long, he said,

"I'm surprised you even managed to find this place. Spring Valley doesn't show up on many maps."

"Hank, my—my late husband—his parents live in Glen Rock, not too far from here. I fell in love with the area the first time we visited. It seemed just like the place I wanted to live when I was a kid. Somewhere far away from the busy city life, with land and animals to tend…"

Her voice drifted away, as if she was picturing the ranch, not as it was, but as she must have imagined it when she was little. She seemed so sincere, so hopeful, that he knew he'd do whatever he could to help make that dream a reality.

Then she started walking again and he followed. In what felt like too short a time, they had finished most of the fence and then just had the paddock left. He wished there were more fence to saunter along, some other reason to dawdle outside. There was something calming, *right*, about strolling out there with Cassie and her boys.

"Have you lived here your whole life?" she asked, pulling him out of his reverie.

That simple question was always a difficult one to answer, and even though he felt like Cassie was a person he could confide in, he wasn't ready to explain the whole situation to her. He stuck with his honest-but-short response, hoping she wouldn't ask for more details. "No. I lived in San Diego for a while when I was little."

"Surfer-turned-cowboy, huh?" she said with a smile.

Her fun tone made him want to joke with her, but he couldn't bring himself to do more than give her a small smile. The image of his father teaching him to surf always brought with it an unpleasant ache in his chest. Despite all the extreme sports he'd tried as an adult, he'd never been able to get back on a surfboard. "Something like that" was all he said.

She seemed to sense his unwillingness to discuss his life in San Diego, because she didn't ask him anything more about his childhood.

CASSIE WASN'T SURE if she was happy or not that the walk was over as they finished the loop around the paddock. It was hot, and she was looking forward to the cool and shade of the house, and to an icy drink, but she couldn't help but wish she and Brock were still ambling on beside each other. He somehow managed to set her on fire and soothe her soul at the same time, and she worried the feeling would disappear once they were back in the house, away from the great expanse of land that surrounded them.

They stopped walking, and Cassie lingered an extra moment. Brock made no move toward the house, either, and they stood there quietly as the boys ran inside.

"So, what's the verdict? How much do I need to replace?" she asked, not yet ready to go inside.

Brock smiled at her, and she felt her heart thump. "Not much, actually. It's better than I would have expected, and the paddock shouldn't take more than a bit of lumber and a few hours' work before it's ready to hold your horses."

Cassie felt relief course through her. Maybe she

would be able to make this work, prove to herself that she could do it.

She looked into his eyes, and the heat around them grew even thicker with unsaid thoughts. Cassie was wondering what it would be like to kiss him when the slam of the screen door came as a welcome diversion. She turned toward the house, creating distance between her and the smoldering man beside her.

Both of her boys were running across the golden grass toward her, leaving a woman standing on the back porch. Cassie squinted in the bright sunlight to see who it was.

Carter skidded in front of her, already talking. "Momma, Miss Emma is here. She brought a pie. She said it was for dessert, but can we have some now? Please?"

"Is that Emmaline Reynolds?" Brock asked from behind her.

Something like jealousy popped up in Cassie, but she quickly tamped it down. She had no call to feel possessive about Brock, she reminded herself. He could date Emma all he wanted.

She couldn't stop herself from saying a quick prayer that he wouldn't, though.

"I haven't seen her since grade school. Didn't even know she still lived here. You sure make friends fast," Brock commented.

Her mood suddenly lifted, she flashed him a smile. "When you have a sweet tooth and two young kids and you move to a town with one bakery, you get to know the owner of said bakery very quickly. Especially when the boxes of kitchen supplies go missing for a week. We've also made friends with the owners of the pizza place and the café."

Brock chuckled, the sound reverberating through her body, and his grin caught her off-guard, turning her legs to jelly. She started to regret saying something amusing, looking at him and having a sex drive at all, because this man was certain to be her downfall if a laugh and a smile could do all that to her. Apparently not noticing her discomfiture, he said, "I'm going to go do another check of the paddock real quick, just to be sure we didn't miss anything, and then it's probably best we take a break anyway. You'd be surprised how fast the heat can get to you."

It wasn't the heat that was getting to her, but she wasn't about to say that.

"I'll go see what Emma wants. Come on in whenever you're done," she said to him as she turned away.

She was going to need to be very careful around Brock McNeal.

At the back porch, Emma smiled at her friend. "I came to tell you that I need some more of your business cards to put by the register, because people have been taking them left and right. You should expect to start getting calls for appointments any time now. My neighbor, Mrs. Edelman, asked me to bring her in just as soon as you're open for business. In fact, I'm not working the day after tomorrow, if you'll be ready by then"

Cassie couldn't believe it. "I may not have my office perfect yet, but I'd be happy to meet her then, if that works for you."

Emma nodded, satisfied. "And you really ran through all those cards?" Cassie couldn't help but asking.

"What can I say? People here are excited to have a doctor in town," Emma responded.

Cassie had given Emma a stack of cards only a few days before, in the hopes that she could start meeting with patients as soon as the office was completed. If they were gone already, and if she had her first appointment lined up, her practice might get a running start after all, and she would be able to pay for whatever new expenses cropped up.

Emma's voice broke through her thoughts, bringing her back to reality. "Also, I brought you an official 'welcome to the neighborhood' pie. And it's a 'thanks for treating my burns' pie and an 'I'm glad to have a friend who's also the town doctor and plan to keep her very happy' pie, too."

Emma tilted the pie in her hands so Cassie could see the laced top, beautifully browned with dark berries peeking out and sugar crystals sprinkled on top. The sight made Cassie's mouth water. She laughed. "Pies convey a lot of meaning, huh?"

Emma shrugged. "I just want you to know that I'm glad you moved here, Doc. You have great timing."

When Emma had burned her arm badly the week before while Cassie and the boys were at the bakery, Cassie was happy to help treat the wound. That and Emma's amazing cinnamon rolls had started a quick friendship, one that Cassie was very grateful for in her new life.

"Your very meaningful pie looks amazing, Emma," she responded, inhaling the wafting smell of pastry and berries.

"I thought you could probably use a treat, but," Emma added, nodding her head toward Brock in the distance, "it seems like you already have a sweet treat here. Who is that?" she asked in a gossipy whisper.

Cassie looked toward Brock, whose muscles looked almost heavenly in the bright sunshine as he moved about the paddock that would one day hold her horses. "It's Brock McNeal. His parents live next door and he's giving me a little help fixing this place up. He said he knew you from school."

Emma whistled a low note and leaned back against the doorjamb. "Brock McNeal. I haven't seen him since we were kids. He did a great job growing up."

Cassie ushered Emma into the cool, dim kitchen, where they put the pie on the counter. Emma kept looking out the window at Brock, leaving Cassie feeling more agitated than she'd like. "Did you two date in high school? I imagine everyone in such a small town must've gone out with each other at some point. Unless you're related, of course," Cassie said as nonchalantly as she could.

Emma's head whipped around to stare at Cassie, and she gave her a conspiratorial smile. "No, we never dated. I moved away in middle school and only came back two years ago to start the bakery. I missed my chance, I guess."

Cassie tried to pretend she didn't hear what her

friend was implying. "Let me take a look at your burn. I want to make sure it's healing."

Emma's expression made it very clear she wasn't fooled by the change of subject. Cassie couldn't help but laugh when Emma rolled her eyes and crossed her arms, refusing to cooperate until she was given more details. "He's attractive," Cassie admitted, "but I've got my boys and too much to do around here as it is. Brock's just helping me fix up the ranch. Nothing romantic going on. I'm not about to start any messy relationships."

"A messy relationship could be really fun," Emma said, slipping Cassie a wink and rolling up her sleeve. Cassie inspected the nearly healed burn, happy with its progress and that Emma didn't push the subject of Brock McNeal any further. Cassie was quite aware of how fun a messy relationship with the man could be, and she was determined not to allow that thought to go any further than it already had.

After ensuring herself that Emma had taken care of the burn as directed, Cassie released Emma's arm as Brock came in the door, carrying a couple short planks of wood and a hammer. "Hey, Brock. Long time no see," Emma said.

Brock smiled at her. "Good to see you, Emma. I'd shake your hand, but—" He trailed off, gesturing at the lumber in his arms. "How's your brother?"

"Oh, he's fine," Emma said, leaning against the counter. Cassie couldn't say for sure if Emma was being casual or flirty, and immediately wanted to smack herself on the forehead for even caring. "He's saving lives in Cambodia. Making the rest of us look bad. You know how it is."

Brock chuckled, but this time the feelings it created in Cassie's belly weren't nearly as nice as before. She wished Emma wasn't quite so tall and leggy. Next to her, Cassie felt tiny, almost invisible.

"I know how that is. My sister's the same way," Brock said before turning to Cassie.

When his eyes locked to hers, Cassie's heart began to pound. She suddenly felt anything but invisible. "I'm just going to fix that bunk bed real quick, then I'm going to go home and get cleaned up. Is it okay if I come by in a few hours, though? Once it cools down a bit, I can bring over a crowbar from our place and start tearing out boards in the paddock that need to be replaced."

Cassie felt nearly breathless with his generosity. "You don't have to do all that," she answered, aware that Emma was standing right beside her. "It's too much to ask."

Brock shrugged. "I'm not doing much else but getting in my ma's way. It's nice to feel useful. And those kids won't be able to properly settle into their room until that bed's safe enough to withstand a hurricane. I'm guessing they'll push that furniture to the limits as much as the Wilson boys did."

Cassie returned his smile. She had been worried about the same thing, and her heart filled with gratitude. "Thank you so much, Brock," she said, putting a hand to her chest in a show of earnestness.

It was only when Brock's ears reddened slightly that she realized where her unconscious gesture directed his gaze, and she quickly dropped her hand to her side. Intensely aware that Emma was watching, Cassie tried to lighten the mood. "I'll need to make another stack of pancakes to thank you. And you're welcome to a slice of delicious pie, thanks to Emma," she finished, pointing toward the dessert.

Brock smiled at her. "Can't say no to that," he responded. "I'll just go take care of that bunk bed and then I'll be out of your hair for a few hours."

With that, he was out of the kitchen. Cassie waited, listening for Brock's footsteps to fade.

It was only after he was definitely out of earshot that Cassie turned to Emma, hoping her friend had missed that short moment of tension—if that was what it was, which Cassie had probably misinterpreted anyway—and had only seen an innocent conversation. Cassie was proud of herself. Really, she thought, Emma couldn't possibly have cause to think their relationship was anything but neighborly.

Which is all it is and will ever be, a stern voice inside her scolded. The reminder didn't cheer her.

Emma looked at Cassie and shrugged. "Fair enough," she said. "I've never had luck with love anyway. Maybe you will."

"What does that mean?" Cassie asked, praying Emma didn't mean what Cassie knew she meant.

"Don't even try that," Emma responded, wagging her finger at Cassie. "I know when a guy's hooked. His eyes were locked on your face that whole time, except for when he was distracted by your…hand," she said, wiggling her eyebrows suggestively. "He could hardly manage a glance at me, and he didn't even look at my pie, which is a first."

"Maybe he doesn't like pie," Cassie suggested, trying to brush away Emma's insinuations.

Her friend snorted in response, as if the very idea was preposterous. "Well, I need to get back to the shop, but I expect to hear more about Brock McNeal the next time I see you."

After giving Emma another stack of business cards and saying goodbye, Cassie went to Zach and Carter's room. She walked in to find the boys at opposite ends of the bunk bed, pushing and pulling at it with all their might, giggling hysterically in the process. Brock was standing a few feet away, watching with his hands on his hips.

None of them seemed to notice her arrival, so she stood in the doorway and watched as the boys collapsed on the floor, laughing breathlessly.

"I told you that it wouldn't budge an inch," Brock told the boys.

Cassie moved forward into the room and looked closely at the bed, noting the boards Brock had used to steady the wobbling top bunk. Before she could think of what to say, Zach and Carter were on her, pulling her over to show her exactly what Brock had done to make their bed safe.

She allowed herself a quick glance in his direction to find him suddenly looking slightly awkward, and before she could say anything he hooked his thumb toward the door. "I'm going to go home to wash up and change, but I'll be back this afternoon."

Hardly waiting for a nod from her, he strolled out of the bedroom. She faintly heard the front door open and close, and he was gone.

Why had he disappeared so quickly? She hadn't even been able to express her thanks for what he had done for Zach and Carter.

"He's nice," Carter commented, climbing up into his new bed. Cassie had to agree.

Nice, and sexy. And a little bit confusing.

With a deep exhale, she headed to the shower to wash off the sweat from the heat of the day. It also gave her time to think.

Her first thoughts as she stepped into the water strayed to Brock. Showering. With her. Emma's words rang in her head. *I know when a guy's hooked...*

The idea made her stomach flutter with excitement. She immediately shoved her head under the cool spray, biting back her sexual frustration.

Why, why did the man willing to help her need to be quite so perfect?

Men weren't an option right now, Cassie knew, but oh, man, if they were, she knew right where she'd go.

Cassie sighed and turned off the water, feeling cleaner but still very unsatisfied.

She would need to be careful if she was going to avoid rumors getting around town that she and Brock were an item. She didn't want the boys to hear anyone suggesting that she might be replacing their daddy.

She could just imagine the whispered talk, the way people would look at her, wondering how much was true...

She'd been through that too recently for the idea of it starting all over again to sit well.

And if she knew Emma at all from their short friendship, she guessed talk would be all around town in a matter of days. The thought made her skin crawl.

This time, though, she could at least make sure the rumors had no truth behind them, no teeth to sink into her and hurt her.

Chapter Five

"Thanks, Diego," Brock said into his phone as he sat on his childhood bed. "I'll let Cassie know you guys will buy the hay."

"No problem. She's doing us a favor, really," Brock's adopted brother answered. "Tomorrow when we get into town, Jose and I will drop by to meet her and hammer out the details."

They said their goodbyes and Brock hung up. Since he'd been home, he had eaten, showered and called his brothers about the hay. He looked at the clock and knew he should kill some more time before heading back to Cassie's.

Brock glanced around the room, at his high school rodeo trophies, snapshots of him with his friends and siblings, and a picture of him bungee jumping when he was seventeen—Ma had been so mad when she'd found out, but she still didn't have the heart to get rid of the picture, apparently. All these relics of his life in this home hardly registered, though. His mind was listening to the slow ticking of the clock, and thinking of the woman a house away.

After deciding to wait another half hour, Brock stood

and paced as best he could in the cramped room. He probably wouldn't have lasted another thirty seconds, but luckily, his phone buzzed in his pocket. He looked at the screen to see that Jay, one of his rodeo buddies, was calling him.

He swiped the screen and put his phone to his ear. "Hey, Jay. Did you make it in the money?"

He had left too early from the last rodeo to see Jay ride, but his friend was one of the best bull riders on the circuit, and he was sure the man had done well.

"Second place," Jay said. "Your uncle was hopping mad that you didn't get a chunk of the purse."

Brock shrugged, even though his friend couldn't see it. He'd expected as much. "Uncle Joe is hopping mad about half the time. I'll do better in the next one," he added, more for himself than anything.

"Speaking of the next one," Jay said, no doubt getting down to his reason for calling, "you're going to the rodeo in Glen Rock, right?"

That was the one coming up in two weeks. It was about the closest big rodeo Spring Valley had all year. "Yeah, I'll be there," Brock said, wondering where this was going.

"Well, I found out there are some abandoned mines about an hour out of town, and I've been looking into mining exploration. How about a group of us head there and check them out on our way out of town the day after the rodeo? I'll bring rappelling gear and flashlights. I've been reading up on it, and we might be able to find something down there. I've heard of people stumbling onto rubies the size of your fist in abandoned mines."

Brock seriously doubted they'd be finding any giant rubies, but Jay's plans always turned into great stories, and it would give Brock something to do after the rodeo. He had a feeling he might need something big to keep his mind off leaving Spring Valley. And the people that resided there. "Sounds like a plan," Brock responded.

"Great!" Jay said. "I'll see you at the rodeo!"

"See you," Brock said, hanging up and sliding his phone into his back pocket.

He sat back down on the bed, resolved to follow through with this new, likely dangerous, plan. It was good to have a reminder about what kind of life he was living. Anything that happened between him and Cassie couldn't last. He'd have to move on eventually, and what better way to show that than to jump into a mine the day after he left town?

Sure, Cassie was beautiful, and interesting, and seemed to have an amount of inner strength that intrigued him. Something about her pulled at him with an intense attraction he'd never experienced before. But she also had children and the kind of settled home life he wasn't looking for and didn't want. He'd worked so hard for so long to keep all that out of his future, and he couldn't just chuck it away now.

He was a rodeo bull rider, a thrill-seeker, a free spirit.

Even though it had only been five minutes since his decision to wait another thirty, Brock gave up and pushed his cowboy hat onto his head as he went downstairs. After grabbing a crowbar from the storage shed beside his parents' barn, Brock set off for the ranch next door.

As he tromped across the lush expanse that separated his parents' home from Cassie's, Brock took a deep breath of the warm air, the smell of dust and grass as familiar as an old friend. The old Wilson place stood out against the mountain backdrop like something in a painting: the cozy ranch in the Texas countryside.

Cassie's smile disrupted his thoughts once more. Despite his reservations, maybe he would ask her out… He couldn't offer her more than a nice night out or two, but he wasn't sure he could withstand the pull between them altogether. But, he reminded himself, he really should wait a bit longer. Make sure she knew that he was there to help her, whether or not they were having fun on the side. That would give him a bit more time to think this through.

Brock knocked on the door, confident that he had a solid game plan, only for everything to fall away the moment the door opened.

Cassie stood there, her hair still slightly damp from her own shower, so fresh and enticing. "Thanks for coming over again. Do you mind if we go get paint instead of starting on the paddock? I'm going to meet a patient the day after tomorrow, so I'll need to paint it tonight or tomorrow morning."

It was as if, in the small space of time they were apart, he'd convinced himself he could be patient around her. But seeing her now, the attraction was hitting him full force. The look of excitement on her face just added to it.

Before his brain could stop him, he stepped forward and kissed her, his lips touching hers lightly at first, then harder when she responded. Her hand slipped around his neck to pull him against her. For a long moment, they melted together. When they finally broke apart, though, the expression on her face wasn't promising. "Go out with me tonight," Brock blurted out.

Her expression only worsened, but there was nothing he could do now except continue on. "Nothing serious. I'm going back on the circuit in a couple weeks. I just thought that we…"

He trailed off. Before she said anything, he knew what her answer would be. "I can't," she said, shaking her head. "Not with the boys, and Hank—"

She paused, as if searching for the right words, but he knew he didn't want to hear them. She was still in love with her valiant police officer husband, and any physical attraction she had for him wasn't going to change that. He didn't need to make her say it. Before she could speak again, he shrugged and smiled, trying to hide his disappointment. "Hey, it's no big deal. We can be friends, right?"

"Right," she responded, but she still looked uncomfortable.

He wanted to do something to *show* her he was still willing to help her fix up her place. "We should get to the hardware store. If we don't dawdle, we can get your office painted today, and then you'd be able to see patients tomorrow, if you want."

Cassie nodded, though she still seemed lost in thought.

"Let's take my truck so we can haul the lumber you'll need for the fence and paddock, too," he told her.

Cassie finally seemed to come back around, though her eyes wouldn't exactly meet his. "That sounds like a great idea. Does your truck have a backseat for the boys?" she asked.

At least she wasn't mad at him, he thought with relief. "Yep, plenty of room," he said.

"I'll get the boys ready, then," she said, half turning away from him, back toward the dim interior of the house.

Brock looked back to his parents' house, where his truck shone in the driveway. "I'll go get my truck and meet you back here in a few minutes."

Cassie nodded and disappeared into the house. Brock started down the steps after setting the crowbar out of the way on the porch. With the change of plans, he wouldn't be using it quite yet, but it didn't make sense to carry it all the way back when they would need it another day.

Brock strode quickly back the way he had just come a few minutes before, steering himself toward the driveway this time. He berated himself the whole way. What had he been thinking, kissing her like that?

Brock knew the answer. He'd been thinking she was interesting and smart and all kinds of sexy. But that didn't change the fact that he'd known better than to do that. It seemed Cassie wasn't the only one who was impulsive. She bought a ranch, he kissed women without thinking.

Well, one woman.

At least now he knew he didn't have a shot with her, even if she seemed to feel the same electricity he did. She may have gotten caught in the moment, but the look of instant regret on her face was all he needed to know that it wouldn't be happening again. If she was still loyal to her husband's memory, he couldn't begrudge her that. So they would just be friends.

Brock hopped in his truck and drove the short stretch of road to Cassie's house. By the time he got there, she and the boys were bustling down the porch steps.

As soon as he opened the vehicle door, he could hear the boys chattering excitedly about the prospect of riding in a big cowboy truck. He smiled as they tried to climb in, struggling with the height of the cab.

"Here," he said, lacing his fingers together and kneeling down to create an extra step for them.

Once the boys were in, he looked at Cassie, who was standing there. She was giving him a small smile that he couldn't interpret. "Thanks for this," she said to him.

He wasn't sure what to say. Would things be too awkward between them now?

Brock felt a little sheepish. "I want you to know that I'm not a jerk, and I'm sorry if I came off as one earlier."

Cassie moved as if she was going to put her hand on his arm, then seemed to rethink it and dropped her arm to her side. "I don't think that, Brock."

God, he wanted to kiss her again. He turned to the truck to get away from her beautiful eyes and realized the boys were crowded with his duffel bags from time on the rodeo circuit. By the time he'd moved the bags into the truck bed, Cassie had already gotten in and closed the door. He wasn't sure if he was grateful or disappointed that their moment was over.

CASSIE SETTLED INTO the passenger seat of Brock's car, her heart pounding. She still felt aflutter from the scene at the door, though dissatisfied at the same time. That kiss. Oh my. And then he had asked her out.

And she'd said no.

Oh, she wished she could have said yes. She wanted nothing more than to kiss him again, press her body against his. As she sat beside him in the front seat, she could almost feel the energy between them, hot and thick. She could imagine laughing with him at a restaurant, touching his hand, talking with him as he walked her to her door, kissing him again and again in the country moonlight.

But her boys jabbering excitedly in the backseat reminded her again that now just wasn't the time to start dating. They were still so young, and they'd lost their father so recently. She had to be a mother first, a doctor second and a rancher third. Being a single woman was so far down on the list it didn't even rate a mention.

"I spoke with my brothers," Brock said, breaking the silence and dragging her back into the moment. "They're happy to buy your hay. They wanted to know if they could drop by tomorrow to see it and talk to you about prices."

Relief washed through Cassie, both for a safe topic of conversation and the possibility of one big worry to be solved so quickly. "Absolutely. Thanks for calling them," she responded, not sure what else to say.

Brock shrugged, though he seemed pleased. "They were planning on visiting anyway, and you'll be doing them a service, really. Getting a new business off the ground is no easy feat."

"What did you say their business was? Selling animals?" She was interested, but mostly she just wanted to keep the conversation light and flowing.

"Sort of," he answered. "They own stock—bulls, broncs, a few calves—and they rent them out on the rodeo circuit."

Cassie's eyes widened at the news. She'd never been to a rodeo, but was looking forward to changing that very soon. She was a cowgirl now, after all.

"I imagine you and your siblings have been to quite a few rodeos, living around here," she said.

Brock chuckled. "More than you can imagine. Amy, my sister, rode in the junior rodeo. She only gave it up when she became a journalist and started traveling the world."

"And you?" she prompted.

He had said he was on the circuit when the boys asked what his job was, and again during the recent scene on the porch that she was trying to forget. She wasn't positive, but she thought she'd heard that phrase in connection to rodeos.

"I ride bulls on the circuit. I travel around from one rodeo to the next and compete," he explained, his eyes on the road.

Cassie hadn't expected that. She was aware of the fact that some people out there hopped on the back of giant twisting animals for a living, but she'd never actually met one.

She tried to focus on the danger of it, to remind herself to keep her distance from this man.

But she could just imagine him, using every one of his very noticeable muscles as he defeated a crazed bull in a battle of strength and wills. The picture sent a thrill through her.

Cassie shook her head slightly at her own silly imagination. If they were going to be friends, she would need to avoid picturing him in that romantic way. Or maybe theirs would need to be a very distant friendship. Just close enough to work together on her house and barn. After that, it would probably be best if they didn't see each other much. Like a mantra, she repeated the important things: children, patients and horses.

Horses. "Oh, shoot," she said aloud, "we were planning to go and visit our horses tomorrow morning. Will your brothers be able to come in the afternoon?"

Brock nodded. "That should be fine." Then he added. "Since we're getting the lumber today, I can work on the paddock while you're out, if that's okay."

She melted a little. Even though she'd turned him down, he was still willing to work so hard to help her.

She had spent years married to someone selfish, and now she'd finally found a nice man she couldn't have. Thanks, Destiny.

"That would be wonderful," she said. Before she could think things through, she blurted out, "Unless you want to come with us?"

She wanted to slap her forehead. Why was she putting herself into these situations? She should be spending *less* time with him, not *more*!

But it was too late now. Her impulsiveness had gotten the better of her once again, so she might as well go all in. "I don't know much about horses and would appreciate having them looked over by someone with a practiced eye," she said.

He gave her a little smile that wiped away the nagging voices inside her. She knew exactly why she asked him to come—she couldn't help but want to be around him.

"Can't say no to spending some time around horses," he answered.

Cassie spent the rest of the drive amazed at the human capacity for conflicting emotions.

Finally, they reached the hardware store, to Cassie's relief. The large building was a reminder that she had more important things to do than fight herself over Brock. They all climbed out of the truck and headed inside.

Now she could think about those other things: paint for her doctor's office, lumber for her fences, and plenty of other items she didn't even know she needed. Even the worries at the cost of it all seemed preferable to thinking about Brock.

Zach and Carter looked around them at the large store, and Cassie could see their fingers itching to touch everything they could reach, the more dangerous the better. "How about we go pick out paint?" she asked. When they seemed disappointed, she added, "You two can paint your room any color you can both agree on."

With that, they were hopping excitedly toward the paint swatches, already arguing about what color to choose. Cassie followed them, feeling Brock beside her, but not looking at him. "You're really going to let them pick *any* color they want?" Brock asked, sounding amazed.

Cassie nodded, keeping her eyes trained on her sons. "They'll have a hard time agreeing, and Zach will keep Carter from choosing something too crazy. He won't want anything too bright."

At least she could feel confident about one aspect of her life right now. She knew her boys.

They walked through the store, looking like a happy family on an outing, Cassie knew. She tried to brush the idea away. This was time for work. She turned her mind, instead, to choosing exactly the right color for her office.

Cassie followed the boys into the paint section and felt immediately overwhelmed at the number of choices. Giant sections of hundreds of colors surrounded her, each section a different name brand. She didn't even know where to start, and the only name she recognized was some of the brands boasted ultra-expensive collections.

Beside her, Brock pointed out a name she didn't recognize. "I suggest getting one of these ones. They make good paint at a decent price. We can find the right one to spruce up the fencing and keep it water-tight here, too."

With her choices narrowed to a much more manageable hundred-or-so options, Cassie followed Brock and started pulling out paint cards to consider. Soon she had a dozen or more in her hands, from periwinkle to sky blue to mocha to gentle fawn. She could hear Zach and Carter arguing over colors, and she could see Brock out of the corner of her eye considering which dark brown would match best, but she was mostly, blessedly, absorbed in the choices in front of her.

"Hmm. Tough choice," Brock said, sidling so close to her that she could smell his cologne or aftershave or whatever it was that made him smell so darn good.

Damn. Her mind was now 100 percent on him, her libido firing up and demanding action, the memory of them on the porch only compounding the problem. She forced herself to stay still, her eyes on the colors in front of her, even though she was no longer really seeing them.

As if Brock could feel the intensity of her desire, he stepped back a little and cleared his throat.

Cassie kept her eyes on the squares of color, purposely avoiding looking at him. "I'm just not sure what would be best."

Brock leaned back for a second, putting his hand on his chin as he considered. Then he leaned forward and plucked out two of the colors: a buttery yellow and a bold blue. As he did so, his fingers grazed hers, and she pulled back as if singed and looked up at him, the absolute wrong thing to do, she realized. The dark blue of his eyes threatened to suck her in.

He held up the colors he'd chosen as if they were a type of protection from her, and she reined in her thoughts, turning her attention to the swatches.

"I think either of these would go particularly well with the furniture," he said, his voice sounding strained. "But any of the colors you picked would be fine, honestly."

She had to agree with him. After a quick inner debate, she chose the blue. "The yellow reminds me too much of a nursery," she explained, not mentioning that the blue reminded her of his entrancing eyes.

Brock didn't respond, and when she saw how awkward he'd become once again, she scolded herself for bringing up babies with a man who didn't particularly like children.

It didn't stop her from picturing him in a butter-yellow nursery, holding a little baby in his arms, though. She gave herself a little shake and spoke, hoping to clear the air. "Did you find something for the fence?"

He held up the brown swatch and she smiled. It might not have been too exciting for some people, but it was the color a fence and paddock on a working ranch should be, and that made her happy. They brought the colors up to the paint-mixer and placed the orders. When they finished, Brock said, "You should also think about what color you want the barn to be. You'll need to repaint the whole thing at some point."

He didn't have to say that it would need to wait until after he was gone. There simply wasn't time while he was in town to get that done on top of everything else. The thought made her sad, but she tried to ignore it. "Hmm… I might go for a white barn," she said, picturing the beautiful white against the deep greens and browns of the surrounding landscape.

Brock nodded. "It would be a pain to keep looking bright, but white barns are nice," he said.

Before she could comment again, Zach and Carter ran up, smiles on their faces.

"We chose a color!" Zach said, holding out the chosen swatch.

Cassie looked down at the lurid green and groaned. "Really?" she asked. "This is what you both want?"

"Look at the name!" Carter said, "The nice man helped us read the names," he explained, pointing to the tiny words on the bottom of the swatch.

Dragon scales.

Cassie looked over to see the clerk who had helped them. He gave her a pained smile—apparently he realized too late the problem with letting two little boys know that a color had the word "dragon" in the name. She could hear Brock laughing behind her. "Well, that backfired," she said to him, handing the color swatch over to be mixed. She had promised, after all.

After the paint, it was quick work to walk into the lumber area and find the right size boards, then get a small crew of workers to haul the lumber to Brock's truck. Cassie went to the checkout line with several cans and buckets of paint, the necessary accompanying items, plus a ticket for the lumber. Thankfully, the purchase went through without too hard a hit on her bank account.

When she slid into Brock's truck, a feeling of triumph washed over her. She hadn't done anything too stupid, like kiss him again, and her finances were working out better than she'd hoped. She was going to make it through all this.

She could see herself and her boys, snug in their new home, with the horses in the barn and her patients getting the help they needed in her little examination room. They would all be just fine, even when Brock left for his rodeo circuit.

But first, they would paint her doctor's office together, and she held on to that thought as they drove back home.

Chapter Six

Brock and Cassie looked around the little office with pride. The walls shone with wet paint, and they were both splattered head to toe in it, too, but the task was complete.

Brock knew he should leave now that the job was done, but he waited a few extra seconds anyway.

Zach and Carter, whom Cassie had sent to work in their room rather than have them make an even bigger mess of the paint than the grown-ups, rushed into the room and started tugging at their mother's arms. "Momma, come see all the work we did!" Carter shouted, trying to get her out of the room.

"All our toys are put away and everything," Zach added.

Cassie groaned and leaned against the doorjamb. "Give me a second, boys. Mom's been working very hard all day."

"What're we going to have for dinner?" Zach asked, sounding concerned.

Carter nodded. "I'm hungry."

Cassie ran her hands over her face and through her hair, and Brock's heart went out to her. She seemed even more weary than he felt. "Okay," she said at last, "first I'll figure out food, then you can show me all the work you did. Sound good?"

The boys looked disappointed, and Brock could sense that they really wanted her to see what they had done. "If you're happy with sandwiches or pasta, I can work on food while you go with the boys," he suggested.

Cassie looked as if she was about to object, so he said, "It's purely selfish, I assure you. I'm starving and you promised me dinner and that pie, which is sounding mighty delicious right about now." He continued, "We need to have a meal before we have dessert, right?"

Cassie gave him a half smile, making it clear she saw right through him, but all she said was, "That's right. No dessert before dinner in this house."

Brock smiled. "Well, then, I best rustle up some grub."

"You talk like cowboys on TV," Zach said, looking at Brock in awe.

Brock tipped the cowboy hat he'd just placed on his head after retrieving it from the living room, where he'd stowed it for safety earlier in the day. "You stick around here for a bit, pardner, and you'll start talking like that, too."

Zach's eyes widened in amazement. He stared at Brock for another moment, trying to absorb the idea of him speaking like a cowboy, before following his mother and twin toward his bedroom. Brock chuckled and went to the kitchen. They were good kids, all right.

After a quick inventory of ingredients, he got a pot

of water and an oiled pan heating on the stove, then gathered tomatoes, an onion and some cloves of garlic, and started chopping.

He dropped spaghetti noodles into the boiling water and slid a pile of chopped onion and tomato into the hot pan, where they sizzled as they began to cook. Cassie walked in, telling the boys how impressed she was with their progress. The boys beamed.

When she came up beside Brock to look into the pot on the stove, he risked a glance at her before going back to chopping more tomatoes. She just looked so damn *kissable*, even when she was worn out from a hard day's work, her dark hair in disarray around her face, and a smudge of blue paint on her chin.

Brock shifted, uncomfortable as Cassie leaned in even closer, sniffing the tomatoes in the pan. "Smells great," she commented.

"Pasta pomodoro, or, in layman's terms, spaghetti and tomato sauce."

Cassie chuckled low in her throat, sending a thrill through him. "Not exactly cowboy fare," she said.

He smiled, but kept his eyes on the tomatoes as he finished chopping. "Well, you don't have any chicken to fry or ribs to barbecue, so I fell back on bachelor fare. Easy, cheap and good."

"I'm *so* hungry!" Carter exclaimed, breaking into their tête-à-tête.

Cassie turned to her son, "That was a little rude, buddy," she said.

"Sorry," he responded, sounding so contrite that Brock wanted to laugh.

"I'm hungry, too, but we need to wait for everything to cook. What can we do while we wait?" she asked.

The boys jumped up, shouting over each other about plates and washing hands, and suddenly there was a flurry of activity behind him.

Cassie came back to where Brock stood, stirring the sauce. "Sorry about that," she told him as she pulled out a noodle to check.

Brock shook his head. "Nothing to apologize for."

He was actually amazed. Cassie made raising children look so easy.

She took the pot of noodles off the stove and strained out the water, dumping them in a large bowl and bringing it over to Brock so he could put the sauce on top. Just as they had with the bookshelves and the painting, the two of them worked together seamlessly. In no time, they were all sitting around the table, everyone eating with the speed of the hungry and tired.

"'S'good," Carter mumbled through a mouthful of noodles.

The rest of the family grunted in agreement.

Once the spaghetti was gone and their hunger abated, Brock leaned back, letting his body relax. He could see the pinks of the sky through the windows, and knew the sun had gone down and he'd spent nearly the entire day with Cassie, despite his inward insistence that he help her while having as little contact with her as possible.

Well, at least if he worked longer days, he could always finish early and spend the last days of his visit to Spring Valley Cassie-free, right?

He couldn't fool himself into believing that was a

possibility, though. He knew that he would find *something* around that place to fix up until the day of the rodeo. Even then, it would probably feel like it was too soon.

But for today, at least, he had gone beyond an acceptable visit, and he should leave Cassie and her children in peace to spend the rest of their evening as a family. Without him.

"How about some pie?" Cassie asked him.

"Sure," Brock answered as he began to clear the table.

Well, he couldn't leave until after pie, right?

CASSIE STOOD IN the doorway as Brock walked out. "I'm going to leave my truck here so we can take the lumber out of the bed tomorrow," he said, gesturing to the vehicle piled high with planks of wood.

They'd been so busy with painting that she had totally forgotten about the lumber. "Sounds good," she told him.

With an awkward little wave, as if he wasn't quite ready to leave, Brock turned toward his parents' home and walked away, eventually disappearing into the inky night. Even then she lingered, though she couldn't have explained why. Knowing he would be back tomorrow didn't quite erase the desire to run out into the darkness and bring him back.

The more time she spent around this man, the more things she discovered about him that she liked. Her decision not to date was the right one, of course, but she couldn't stop herself from wishing they had met when the boys were a little older, their father's memory a little more faded.

Cassie shook her head, annoyed with her own train of thought. It was obvious enough to her that he didn't lead a settled life, and never planned to, either. He was a wanderer. Even if the boys were old enough for her to go on dates, Brock would still only be in it for a quick fling, no strings attached.

She came with lots of strings. Two identical strings in particular.

Cassie sighed. There was no hope for it. Brock McNeal was something she wanted that she simply couldn't have.

She shut the door, but it didn't shut out the picture of him kissing her. Or the one of them sitting around the table, eating pie like a family...

She found Zach and Carter in a sleepy heap on the couch and her heart jumped. Even if she couldn't have that picture, she had her boys. "Come on, guys. Time for bed," she said, prodding them gently.

They raised their arms to her, and she lifted them both up, trying to ignore her aching muscles. It wasn't *that* late, but they'd had a long day and were clearly feeling as weary as she was. She carried them to their room and settled Zach onto the lower bunk and Carter onto the upper. She took off their shoes but didn't bother with the rest. The twins curled into their brand-new bed and slept on, oblivious to the world.

BROCK WALKED SLOWLY through the dark country night. The sun had set long before, and a slice of coolness cut the warm summer air. Exhaustion kept him from noticing it much, though.

He tromped upstairs and went immediately into the bathroom, where he scrubbed at the splatters of blue on his hands and arms. Impatient as he was to get to bed, he still wiped down the sink, trying not to leave a trace of paint anywhere. He was a grown man, but he had a healthy fear of his ma's wrath, and nothing could set it off quite like leaving a mess for her to clean.

Brock was so tired. Not just from the day full of fixing and painting and hauling, though that was draining, but from spending the entire time in Cassie's presence.

It wasn't that she was difficult to be around—in fact, it was the exact opposite. He felt *too* comfortable with Cassie. His mind and body yearned for impossible scenarios, which set him constantly on edge around her. After all, he knew that even if she was magically cured of her loyalty for her lost husband and she suddenly decided she wanted nothing more than to be in his arms, there was still the problem of the twins.

Kids made everything more complicated, and he knew he couldn't take over any type of a fatherly role. Not with the kind of life he led.

He thought of Jay and the abandoned mines, and the idea of having children waiting for him to come home sent a shudder through him. What if he never came back?

It was better to have no ties, nobody to hurt.

So all Brock and Cassie could have was a temporary fling, and even that seemed astronomically unlikely at this point. He knew all that. So why was he picturing waking up beside her day after day? Why did he let the twins steal a little bit of his heart when they begged to help their momma prepare her doctor's office?

Brock splashed cold water onto his face, trying to rid himself of those thoughts. It was all moot, anyway, so he might as well let it go. He'd seen her expression after their kiss.

The kiss where she pulled us closer together, a small voice reminded him. Even if she didn't want to date him, she *did* kiss him back. He could still taste her, feel the energy that radiated from her as she responded to him.

Brock walked down the hall to his room, wishing he'd stayed away from Spring Valley and the woman who had so quickly taken over his mind.

"G'night, Brock," Ma called down the hall. "Don't forget, Amy and your brothers will be here tomorrow, so I'll need you home early for a nice big family dinner. No lollygagging over at Dr. Stanford's, you hear?"

Brock felt a retort rise in his throat, but he bit it back. It was certainly true that his mother had been the one to orchestrate his acquaintance with Cassie and offer his help to her, but he didn't need to point that out to her.

There was no reason to snip at his ma anyway. Just because he was grumpy about the unfortunate circumstances that kept him from what he wanted and desired didn't mean he should take it out on the woman who had cared for him nearly all his life.

"Yes, ma'am," he said instead, tilting his hat to her. "G'night."

Ma kept looking at him, and for a moment he thought

she was going to ask about how her matchmaking between him and Cassie was going, but instead she simply nodded and disappeared into the master bedroom.
Brock turned to his own room, feeling relieved; he
didn't have an answer to that question.

Right now, the one and only thing he needed was a
good night's sleep.

CASSIE WOKE UP and stretched, feeling aches in muscles
all along her arms and back. With the all the chores
from the day before, she'd expected as much.

What she hadn't expected was the hours of tossing
and turning as she fought a war about Brock McNeal.
No matter how many times she'd told herself nothing
would happen with him, it didn't stop her body from
complaining about the decision. The more time she
spent around him, the more longing she felt, and their
kiss kept repeating itself over and over in her head. Not
only was that moment mind-blowing and a promise of
so much more to be had, Brock was kind and funny,
not to mention attractive as all get-out.

All she wanted was to keep her hands off him, yet
at the same time, she desired him more than anyone
she'd ever met. Thoughts like that had made it nearly
impossible to sleep.

Cassie felt lighter this morning, however. By the
time the sun had come up, she'd finally decided to allow
herself to accept her feelings for Brock. He wouldn't be
kissing her or asking her out again after already being
shot down, and there was no reason to be stiff and dis-

tant with him, so long as she never went any further again. They had agreed to be friends.

So long as she had too many responsibilities to start up something with the sexy bull rider, why not enjoy light banter with her helpful neighbor?

And speaking of responsibilities…

It was nearly eight, and the fact that she hadn't heard from her sons could either be very good or very bad. Normally they would be banging down the door by now in their excitement to start the day. Cassie groaned and stood up, even though she badly wanted to curl back under her covers.

She slipped on panties and bra—not her sexiest ones, because that would be taking things too far—but on the slinkier side. She told herself it was because the silk felt good against her sore and tired body. Then she dressed in jeans and a blouse that hugged her curves nicely, because it felt good to look good sometimes.

Then she went searching for her sons. She discovered the reason for the twins' absence quickly enough, when she heard thumps and giggles from their bedroom and went to investigate. She opened the door to find Zach hanging on to the railing of the top bunk and swinging himself into the bottom bunk as Carter attacked his brother's legs from the shadows of the lower bunk.

For a second, Cassie considered just closing the door and pretending she hadn't seen what she'd seen. She was sleepy and aching, and being a good parent seemed like a lot of work.

But the doctor in her wouldn't let her walk away.

"What are you two doing?" she asked pointedly, knowing she wasn't going to like the answer.

"Playing on our new bed," Zach explained matter-of-factly.

Cassie softened at their worry-free expressions. "Well, stop playing in ways that might send you to the emergency room. How about we go make some breakfast?"

The boys jumped up and raced past Cassie toward the kitchen. She followed, her heart filled with love for the two rascals.

"Are we going to have pancakes again?" Carter asked once she joined them.

"Cereal today," she answered, glancing at her watch.

They had gotten a late start, and she wanted to get to the horse barn before too much longer. If Brock's brothers were going to be over that afternoon, she wanted to make sure they were back in plenty of time. Plus, she needed to spend some time preparing her office, since Emma had sent a text confirming she'd come by with her neighbor bright and early the next day.

Cassie poured cereal for herself and the boys, then sat down to eat, wondering if Brock would be arriving soon to see the horses with her.

Part of her hoped he would decide not to, but most of her jumped with joy when a familiar knock sounded at the door, as if her thoughts had conjured Brock out of thin air.

"I'll get it!" Carter shouted as he jumped out of his seat and ran to the door.

Cassie put another spoonful of cereal into her mouth

to hide the smile she couldn't stop from spreading across her lips.

Carter came back to his seat. "Brock is here!" he announced unnecessarily, as Brock stepped into the room right behind him.

Cassie looked up from her bowl, trying to keep her face as serious as she could make it, though inside she was grinning like a Cheshire cat. "Back for more punishment, huh?" she asked, thankful she'd decided to let herself flirt without feeling guilty so there was no inward scolding.

Brock gave her the kind of smile that could turn a woman to mush. "I was told we were going to see some horses today. What kind of a cowboy would I be if I passed that up?"

She laughed, unable to contain her glee any longer. She couldn't help how good she felt when he was around, and for the moment the impulsive side of her was winning. She would hate to admit how nice it was to give it free rein.

"Sit down and have some cereal, if you're hungry," she told him, gesturing to the empty seat at the table.

"Oh, I'm fine. Don't trouble yourself," he said, but Zach had already hopped up and grabbed him a bowl and spoon.

She said nothing, just gestured to the empty seat again. He conceded without any more argument. Soon they were all eating, the only sound the clink of spoons on ceramic bowls. Cassie felt more at ease than she had since first meeting Brock. She couldn't pinpoint what, exactly, had happened overnight to so change her attitude toward him.

Perhaps it was that her soreness and exhaustion, along with the excitement of her first patient's looming appointment, had all combined to weaken the tight grip she'd been keeping and made her temporarily foolish. Perhaps the kiss from yesterday had worked some magic on her during the night, creating this newfound inner quiet. Either way, this new, relaxed version of her was exactly what she'd needed.

Cassie smiled down at her bowl again before looking up at the boys and Brock. "Should we go visit some horses?"

BROCK WASN'T SURE what it was, but Cassie seemed different today. More at ease. Was it because she was sure he'd gotten the message when she turned him down yesterday and no longer needed to worry about him making advances? If so, she was right about that, and he was glad the air between them seemed clear.

Brock led the way out the door as Cassie helped the boys put on shoes, but he stopped when he stepped off the porch. His truck was still parked in front of Cassie's house, the back still full of the lumber they'd purchased the day before.

He and Cassie would need to unload it once they got back from the horses, and then they could start on the paddock. Then Brock remembered the crowbar he'd left on the porch, and he decided to grab it and toss it into the truck bed so the boys wouldn't trip over it or anything.

Brock ran up the porch steps to grab it, only to find that Cassie was rushing down them at the same time, the boys right behind her. Brock stopped in his tracks and Cassie came to a halt, too, but the boys weren't paying attention and bowled into her legs, propelling her forward into Brock.

He put his arms out to steady her, catching her before they could tumble down the stairs together. His heart thumped so hard he was sure she could feel it where their chests met. She looked up into his eyes, and without thinking, he leaned toward her. Luckily, she turned away from him to check on Zach and Carter, and he was able to catch himself before doing something phenomenally stupid like kiss her. Again.

Brock forced his gaze from Cassie and instead looked to where her children had been only seconds before. Now they were in a heap on the floor of the porch. Brock started to go to their aid, worried they had gotten injured in the collision or hurt themselves on the crowbar somehow, but then he noticed that they were both doubled up, laughing hysterically.

Cassie put her hands on her hips, but she was smiling. "Now just what exactly is so funny? You're not laughing at *me*, are you?"

The teasing lilt in her voice made Brock grin. He loved seeing Cassie being silly with her boys.

"Carter said we made you into a Momma-sandwich," Zach said at last, gulping for air.

Brock couldn't help but laugh at the humor of four-year-olds. Cassie gave her sons another falsely stern look. "Well, making me into a Momma-sandwich has suddenly turned me into a tickle monster!"

And with that she was on the floor with the boys, all three of them laughing as Cassie grasped at her children, who rolled desperately to evade her fingers.

Brock was laughing so hard his side hurt. He couldn't remember a time he'd laughed that much. Cassie glanced at him with a conspiratorial smile, and for a moment he felt as if he were a part of the scene instead of an outsider.

He didn't want to admit how good that felt.

Cassie stood up, her cheeks red from exertion and amusement, her hair wild and her eyes shining. She was so pretty it hurt.

She looked up at Brock, and his heart stuttered. "You ready?" she asked.

Oh, he was ready, all right. For all sorts of things. It took him a moment to realize that she was asking if he was ready to go visit the ranch where the horses were being stabled. Once he understood, he nodded and followed her down the steps to her SUV. For the moment, he didn't trust himself to speak.

Chapter Seven

Cassie glanced at the back seat to make sure her sons were buckled in, then started the car. As she turned in her seat while she reversed out of the driveway, carefully maneuvering around Brock's loaded-down silver truck, her arm brushed against Brock's muscular bicep. His large frame made the front of the SUV feel too small for comfort, and she was grateful the moment she could settle back into her seat, as far from him as she could manage. In the truck the day before they hadn't felt quite so close, but in her car it was almost…intimate.

And however much leeway she was giving herself to chat and be friendly, intimate was definitely *not* good. She'd tried to hide it, but that moment when she'd been pressed against his chest was almost more than she could handle.

"Where are the horses being stabled?" Brock asked her as they drove away from town, toward some of the larger ranches that dotted this part of the country.

"Stuart Ranch," she answered. "Tom Stuart gave us a good price and won't make me pay if I move them home earlier than expected."

She didn't need to say what needed to get done for that to happen. Brock knew, and she was sure he would do everything in his power to get her animals settled as soon as possible. Another smile touched her lips.

"I've known the Stuarts forever. One of the boys dated my sister for a while. They're good people," he said.

She waited a moment for him to add more details, but the only sounds in the car came from the two boys playing in the back seat. The casual ease at the kitchen table shortly before was threatening to disappear completely, and she wasn't sure what to do to save it.

Luckily, the ranch was close, and soon Cassie gratefully left the confining vehicle. After a quick word with Grandma Stuart—who insisted she watch the twins while Cassie and Brock see to the horses—the pair headed to the large barn.

Horses of all different types walked around the paddocks, munching on hay and relaxing in the morning sunshine.

Tom Stuart was just inside the barn, working with a mare that seemed to be limping slightly. Cassie hoped the animal wasn't too badly injured.

"Brock! Haven't seen you around in a long while," Tom said, moving to shake hands with Brock. "It seems you've met your new neighbor," he added, nodding toward Cassie.

"Came to take a look at her horses. They in here somewhere?" Brock responded.

Cassie couldn't help but compare the two men. Though Tom was handsome in his own right, he couldn't hold a candle to Brock. While both were muscular, Tom was taller, with a more wiry look to him, where Brock was more compact and solid. But that didn't explain what made Brock stand out. He had a spark, a subtle inner liveliness, that called out to her.

Cassie tuned back into reality and the two men before her.

Tom pointed down the length of stalls along one side of the barn. "Cassie can show you where they're stabled, if you don't mind. I need to stay with Sadie here," he said, patting the side of the large mare.

Brock took a step toward the injured animal. "Any idea what's bothering her?" he asked, rubbing the animal's neck, then sliding his hand down to her leg, lifting the hoof and inspecting it.

Cassie watched as Brock and Tom conferred over the horse's hoof. Then Brock let go of Sadie's leg and patted her one last time before turning to Cassie.

She had been so absorbed watching him care for the horse, the concern he showed filling her with if-onlys, that his eyes on her sent a jolt of surprise through her. It took a long moment before she realized he was waiting for her to show him to her horses.

With effort, she tore her gaze from his and, after a quick wave to Tom, turned to the stalls where Rosalind and Diamond were waiting.

"Was it a very serious injury?" she asked.

To her relief, Brock shook his head. "A bruised sole. Not fun, but she'll be right as rain soon enough."

Cassie nodded as she walked up to her horses, turning her attention to the beautiful beasts before her. She was still amazed that they were hers. She'd only visited them twice, and every time she saw the two regal animals, she could hardly believe it.

Before becoming a doctor, she'd wanted to be a veterinarian. Her childhood dream had been to live in the country and own and care for horses. Her mother had disagreed—and while her mother's pushes toward a career as a doctor had been ultimately successful, Cassie had never given up her country dreams. She didn't regret not becoming a vet, but she knew she would have always felt like she'd missed out if she hadn't bought the ranch.

Cassie pressed her face into Diamond's neck, breathing in the scent. Horses of her own, a ranch that was actually coming together and a new life for her and her boys.

If she could keep her nose to the grindstone, she and her boys would be settled and happy here. Then they could be a content little family.

Just the three of them.

Cassie didn't like that there was a drop of sadness in that thought, and she tried to ignore how her heart thumped harder when she saw how kind Brock was to her horses.

She walked up beside him, hoping to learn from him. "Do they have a smooth gait when you ride them?" Brock asked as he rubbed the legs of the sleek chestnut mare.

Cassie felt her cheeks flush with embarrassment. "I've never ridden them," she said. She hated to admit the truth, but she said it anyway. "I haven't ever actually been on a horse."

Brock gave her the look of disbelief she expected, but it quickly shifted to determination. "Well, then, we better saddle them up and take them for a quick ride," he said, moving toward the saddles and tack hanging along the side of the barn. "Tom, you think your ma would be fine with watching the boys for twenty minutes while we let these ladies stretch their legs?" Brock called out to where Cassie could just see Tom in the dim light, still working with Sadie on the far side of the barn.

"She'd keep those two for good and all if she had half the chance," Tom replied.

Brock nodded, as if that settled it, and picked up the first saddle. He made no mention of Cassie's admission, just got to work, for which she was immensely grateful.

Cassie watched carefully as Brock saddled each of the horses, explaining exactly what he was doing as he went. Once he had everything cinched tight and secure, Brock stepped up to Rosalind. "You should take Rosy," he said. "Diamond seems like she might be a little skittish."

He explained to Cassie how to put her foot in the stirrup and swing her other leg over to get onto the horse.

He stood holding the reins, keeping the large animal steady while Cassie attempted to mount her. As she swung herself into the air, she wobbled and instinctively grabbed at Brock's shoulder to steady herself. She could feel his hand on her waist, helping her into the saddle.

By the time Cassie was settled atop the horse and Brock's hand had moved away, she was breathless, and

not from the effort to get up there. It was the second
time that day they'd had far too much physical contact,
and it proved to Cassie that she certainly shouldn't let
it happen again if she wanted to keep her sanity. And
her heart.

She took the reins from him, careful not to touch
him, and instead marveled at the sleek neck of the animal she was now sitting on, touching the horse's mane
with wonder. For the first time in her life, Cassie was
on a horse, reins in hand. This had been a dream of
hers since she was a little girl, and it was finally happening. Excitement and gratitude washed through her.

"Thank you," Cassie told him once he was mounted
on Diamond and leading Rosalind toward the edge of
the ranch.

Brock shrugged, but she could see from his solem-
nity that he understood how important this was to her.
"I was a greenhorn once, too" was all he said.

She sat quietly, reveling in the feel of the large animal shifting beneath her.

Once they were out of the property's fenced enclo-
sure, Brock turned Diamond toward a dirt trail that
wound its way into the distance. Cassie turned Rosy the
same direction to follow him, the way Brock showed
her. When the horse did as directed, Cassie's pride
soared.

"So…" he said.

She knew what he was going to say. "Why did I buy
a ranch and move all the way out here if I'd never even
ridden a horse before?"

He nodded, smiling at her perception.

Cassie sighed and patted Rosy's neck. "I've always lived in the city, and my mother was dead set against me getting on a horse, no matter how much I wanted to, so there was no chance to learn as a kid. When I was an adult and finally had the money, I bought tickets out to Dallas and planned to go for a week at a dude ranch so I could learn how to ride. I was all set to go when I found out I was pregnant. No horses for me. Since then, I'd always been so busy with the twins that the chance never came up again."

Cassie glanced at Brock to see his reaction. He nodded sympathetically. "Well, let's make sure you get comfortable. You'll be doing plenty of riding from now on," he said.

Cassie's heart warmed at the thought.

BROCK WATCHED CASSIE carefully as they first set out, but it quickly became clear that she was a natural on a horse. Soon, he had to avoid looking at her because the swaying of her hips with the horse's gait was more than his body could take. His admiration of her tenacity and refusal to give up on her dream despite the years and obstacles only made her more attractive, and he was having a difficult time resisting her.

"These are good animals," Brock told her. "The Wilsons may have let the place go a little, but they had good taste in horses."

Cassie's smile was such a mix of relief, thankfulness and hope that Brock felt both embarrassed and pleased by her confidence in his assessment. He had seen the look in her eyes the day before, too, when he'd told her the fence didn't need as much lumber and expense as they'd thought.

She clearly had been worrying about finances and her choice to purchase the ranch and move so far from her home, and he was glad he could be the one to ease her concerns. He knew she would fit into her ranch and Spring Valley better than she might give herself credit for.

Their eyes met and held for a moment. Then another.

Brock felt the intimacy settle in around them and instinctively recoiled, shifting his eyes back to Diamond. She had turned him down once before, and he wasn't prepared to get shot down again, so it was best to keep from getting his hopes up. This could easily turn into a romantic horse ride in his mind, and he couldn't allow that. It was important to keep things friendly.

He was starting to hate that word.

"Your top three movies. Go!" he said.

There was a silence, and for a moment he thought she wasn't going to accept the change of mood. Part of him hoped that was true.

Then she said, "Okay, first is *The Count of Monte Cristo*, then *The Terminator* and for the third—" she paused for a second, then spoke all in a rush "—*CuriousGeorgeAVeryMonkeyChristmas*."

"What was that third one?" he asked, risking a glance in her direction.

Her face was red, but she looked at him defiantly. *"Curious George: A Very Monkey Christmas."*

He started to laugh, more at the look on her face than anything else.

"What?" she demanded. "The songs are catchy. And I have little kids."

She laughed, too, and he delighted in the sound of it. "Now it's your turn," she said to him. "And no lying. If *Sleepless in Seattle* is one of your favorite movies, you need to own up to it."

Brock shrugged, still chuckling. "*Sleepless in Seattle* is overrated. I'm a *You've Got Mail* guy myself."

For the next half hour, they talked and laughed about Brock's favorite movies, what they would do if they won the lottery, and what each would bring with them to a desert island.

All too soon, they arrived back at the ranch. Brock hopped off Diamond and moved to help Cassie get down, but before he could, she had dismounted and was standing beside Rosalind, patting the horse with affection. "You're really looking like a cowgirl," he told her.

"Thanks, but don't try to change the topic. You need to give an answer. *One* item to bring to a desert island."

He grinned. "A premade emergency backpack full of food and gear counts as one item. I've bought one before, so I know it exists. Don't get mad at me because my answer was so much better than yours. How would you survive if you just brought a book with you?"

She shook her head at him as they led the horses onto the property. "That's not the point of the question," she said. And, because she was curious, "Why did you need a backpack full of food and gear?"

"I went trekking and mountain climbing with some buddies at the last minute and needed supplies to last a couple of days," he answered.

He didn't mention that the bag had slipped from his arm and smashed on rocks hundreds of feet below on their first ascent, nor how miserable the following days were because of it.

Before she could ask more questions, one of the twins ran out of the house. "I saw you riding the horses from the window! You were gone a long time," he commented.

Brock turned to him, glad he wouldn't need to recount some of his less successful adventures. "Carter, if you were going to an island with no food or water on it, what would you bring in your backpack?"

Carter thought for a moment. "Pancakes," he said.

"Smart man," Brock said, looking at Cassie in triumph.

"Or a boat so I could leave," the boy added.

Cassie grinned at him. "The four-year-old beat you at your own game. You realize that, right?"

Brock shrugged, enjoying the conversation. "He really did. But both of our answers were still way better than a book."

"Who would bring a book?" Carter asked, scrunching up his face to better show his distaste at the idea.

"Okay, smarty-pants," his mom told him, turning him back to the house, "you go back inside. We'll get the horses settled in and be there in a few minutes."

"Can I help with the horses?" he asked, turning to Brock.

Brock was taken aback that the boy was asking him instead of Cassie, but he answered, "Not this time. We want to get them brushed down quickly so we can get back to work on the ranch. Another time, okay?"

Carter nodded excitedly and took off for the house.

CASSIE CONTINUED TO lead Rosalind toward the open barn door, amazed that Carter had asked Brock instead of her. Brock seemed to be thinking the same thing, because as they entered the dim light of the barn, he commented, "I hope what I said was okay with you. I wasn't really expecting Carter to ask me that."

Watching Brock interact in such a comfortable way with Carter had made her heart flip-flop around in her chest, but she tried to keep that out of her voice when she answered. "It was exactly what I would have said."

It was what the father they deserve to have would've said, she thought to herself. She wiped that notion out of her mind as quickly as she could. The twins had her and all the best memories of their dad, and that would need to be enough.

"They're good kids," Brock told her as he led the horses into their stalls, a small smile on his lips.

Diamond and Rosalind settled in, munching happily on the hay.

As Brock handed Cassie a brush and got his own to groom Diamond, he said, "I think Carter is going to be hopping up on one of these horses in no time. Did you see the way he looked at Diamond?"

Cassie had her brush against Rosalind's silky neck, but stopped to turn and looked at Brock. She had suddenly realized something. "How did you know that was Carter and not Zach?"

Brock seemed oblivious to her eyes on him. She could see the smile grow wider across his lips as he brushed down Diamond. "Zach will grow to like them, too, but he's a bit more hesitant, which is probably why he stayed inside. That seems to be a personality trait, don't you think?"

She did, but that didn't answer her question. "No. I mean, how can you tell them apart? You knew it was Carter without anyone telling you."

He turned to look at her, surprised. "They're two different people. They look similar, sure, but they're unique." He hesitated for a moment, then said, "You can tell them apart, can't you?"

Cassie realized she had been staring at Brock like he was crazy and blushed. "I can, but almost nobody else is able to. Even their grandparents and Hank— well, most people can't tell which is which. I was just surprised you were able to."

Brock went back to grooming Diamond, and Cassie got started on Rosalind. After a few seconds of silence, Brock said, "I think people don't really look at identical twins very closely. They just expect them to be the same, so they don't worry about finding their differences."

Cassie found herself nodding, even though she knew he couldn't see her. She had noticed the very same thing.

"My brothers are twins," he went on, "and when we were kids, I noticed that adults didn't try to tell them apart, even though they're separate individuals."

Cassie knew Brock had brothers, obviously, but

he'd never mentioned that they were twins. Trying not to imagine a pair of girls sporting her curly hair and Brock's beautiful eyes, she asked, "Do twins run in your family?"

BROCK KNEW HE could answer without explaining the entire story, but something inside him told him to tell the whole truth. Cassie was bound to find out at some point that he and his siblings were adopted, and he felt like she should hear it from him.

"Actually, they're my adopted brothers," Brock said, keeping his eyes on Diamond's mane. "Ma and Pop never had any kids of their own. They're actually my aunt and uncle."

The repetitive sound of the brush against Rosalind stopped. He didn't turn, but waited for her questions.

After a short silence, Cassie asked, "Do you want to talk about it? You don't have to."

He was so surprised he turned from his task and met her eyes. They were serious but lacked any expression of pity. He knew she must be curious, and he appreciated her ability to not pry. Few people managed that.

Suddenly, without him making the conscious decision to do so, he began talking to her about things he rarely discussed with anyone. "My parents died when I was a kid. A car crash. I moved out here from San Diego to live with my aunt Sarah and uncle Howard right after that. They had adopted Amy, Diego and Jose years before but immediately brought me into the family as if I'd always been a part of it. They saved me, Ma and Pop. Even when things were tough—"

He paused there, not quite sure what he wanted to say. Was he going to tell her about the guilt he'd felt over his parents' death? The dark days he'd never have survived if not for the caring people who treated him with such kindness?

Cassie nodded, seeming to understand, and Brock felt lighter somehow. "Anyway, they gave all of us a home. They're as good a family as I could wish for," he finished lamely.

"I can see that," Cassie agreed, her voice soft, before turning back to her task.

Neither spoke as they finished with the horses then went to find Tom and his mother inside the house. Even when Mrs. Stuart insisted they stay for lunch, Brock and Cassie hardly looked at one another. Finally, they said goodbye to the Stuarts and left with Zach and Carter in tow, each sucking on a candy from their time in the hands of Grandma Stuart.

Brock had known from the first day he'd worked with Cassie that she was a kind, helpful sort of person. Finding out she was a doctor had only confirmed his suspicions. Now, he hoped her big heart wouldn't stop her from treating him the same way she always had. He didn't want or need sympathy or anything else when it came to the death of his parents. He'd had plenty of that growing up.

Mostly, he didn't want to lose the easy way they'd spoken before, and the worry of that possibility made him nervous to say anything at all. Even when he was fighting his attraction for her, there was something about the way they were able to converse that he'd hate to lose. He realized for the first time that they truly had become friends, beyond all the sexual tension and desire, and he didn't want anything to hurt that friendship.

Cassie's voice broke into his thoughts. "Should we start unloading the truck when we get back?"

He said a quick prayer of thanks for the change of topic. "Sure. We can make a pile of the boards out back near the corner of the fence for now, and separate out what we need for the paddock once we start on that. Maybe we'll even be able to get a few sections of it completed before it gets too late, or we could spend some time setting up your office. When did you say you're meeting your first patient?" he asked.

Cassie smiled a little. "Early tomorrow morning. Emma's bringing over her neighbor."

"That's great," Brock said, feeling genuinely happy for her.

She would be up to her ears in patients by the time he left, at that rate.

Cassie didn't look away from the road, but he could see she was happy with the prospect of her first patient. Brock was once again struck with her courage, moving so far away from everything she'd known and starting from scratch.

He imagined her husband's memory played no small part in the decision. If she loved him as much as he suspected, everything in her old life probably reminded her of her loss.

He wasn't sure if he was sympathetic or jealous of a deceased person, but either way it didn't bode well for him.

Chapter Eight

Cassie tried to keep her mind on the road, but her thoughts kept straying back to what Brock had said back in the barn about his past. She ached for the young boy who had lost his parents and everything he'd known, and it gave her a newfound wonder at the strength and humor she found in this handsome cowboy.

She could tell Brock didn't want to hear any of that, though, and she could understand why. He'd probably gotten more sympathy from people than he knew what to do with, and she'd had enough sympathy after Hank's death to last her a lifetime. Just being able to talk about normal life without that pity hovering around the edges was all she'd wanted after his crash, and she bet Brock felt the same way.

So normal was exactly what she'd give him.

Once she parked the car, she enlisted the boys to carry a single piece of lumber between them and readied herself for another bout of heavy lifting. She and Brock gathered the boards and began moving them, load by load, from the bed of the truck, around the side of the house and finally to a growing pile of lumber near the corner of the fence closest to the paddock while the boys "helped" as much as they could.

Cassie's still-sore muscles began to protest almost immediately, but she ignored them. Brock pushed himself, and she didn't complain, happy to be working so hard she couldn't fixate on the way his muscles looked under his shirt or think about the way his lips felt against hers, or how he had opened up and shared his past with her.

None of that was helpful here. She just needed to concentrate on what she was doing.

Once all the lumber was out of the truck and in a big pile, she sat on the boards and sucked in a few slow breaths while the boys dropped their last piece on the ground with a thunk. Brock sat beside her to rest, too, and they watched as the energetic boys tried to make their few boards into a respectable pile like that of the adults. There was a faint ding from Brock's pocket, and he shifted his weight as he attempted to extricate his phone from his jeans.

Cassie could feel the wood heap move beneath her, but it was too late to hop off, and she tumbled to the ground along with the lumber. She heard Brock thud beside her and swear under his breath. She turned toward him, worried he was injured.

He had fallen so close to her that her movements brought her to rest with her chest pressed against his arm. She scrambled away as if he was too hot to touch—which in a way, he was. As if she wasn't having a difficult enough time already. Then she noticed that he was still on the floor, and she dropped to her knees beside him. "Brock? Are you okay?"

He grimaced as he tried to sit up. "Yeah, it's just my back. I tweaked it when I fell."

Cassie offered him her hand, and with her help he was able to stand, though he was obviously still in pain. "It just does this sometimes. Has for years," he said through gritted teeth.

"I think we should take you in for a scan, just to be sure you're fine," she said, her training as a doctor taking over.

Brock shook his head. "I promise, it's not a big deal, Doc. A bit of aspirin and some stretches and I'll be right as rain."

"Can I at least take a look?" she asked, though part of her objected to the idea of seeing more of his body than she absolutely needed to.

She was a doctor, and now was the time to be professional.

Brock glanced at her for just a moment, as if he had some idea what she was thinking, then turned his back to her. She pulled up his shirt and looked at his back, running her hands over his skin, trying to ignore the way his obvious strength made her stomach melt into a puddle.

They were just friends, that was all, she told herself. Yes, he was fit. Yes, if she slid her hands around to his stomach she would likely find six-pack abs that would make her knees go weak. Yes, he could lift her up and pin her against a wall like she'd pictured in her fantasies.

Whoa, Nelly.

She put her hands in her pockets in order to keep herself from touching him any more. "Nothing seems out of place or anything. Likely just a muscle spasm, though you really should get it checked out if it happens often."

Brock pulled down his shirt as he turned, giving her just a glimpse of those abs. Lord, what had she done to deserve this type of punishment? "Sorry about that. You could've been hurt."

She waved away his apology. "It was an accident. You were just checking your phone."

Apparently he'd forgotten about his phone until then, and he pulled it out of his pocket. After a few seconds, he looked up. "My brothers. They were texting to say they're almost here. I should go out and meet them."

Cassie nodded. "Head through the house and get some aspirin. There's a bottle in the cabinet above the kitchen sink. I'll work on stacking the lumber a bit more securely than before," she said, giving him a little smile, which he returned.

She watched him, trying to focus her thoughts and energy into his health and getting the hay turned into bales and sold. The stuff that mattered. Instead, though, her mind kept returning to the feeling of sliding her hands along Brock's skin. When his eyes caught hers, they held for a long moment, and she wondered if he was thinking of the same thing. She waited for him to say something, do something.

Without saying anything, he turned and walked to

the back door of the house. She sat down on what was left of the lumber pile, trying to catch her breath.

"What should we do, Momma?" Zach and Carter asked in unison, clearly itching to help more.

Cassie looked at her hands as she tried to think of something for them to do. The splinters in her palm gave her all the inspiration she needed. "Go grab the tweezers from the drawer under my bathroom sink. I have some splinters, and you probably do, too."

The two boys looked at their hands for a moment, nodded, and took off for the back door. Cassie closed her eyes for a moment, enjoying the moment of silence and calm.

BROCK TOOK A few gulps of water to get down the aspirin and watched as Zach and Carter sprinted past him, bouncing off the walls in their hurry to do whatever mission they were on. Then he walked through the house and out the front door, unsure if he was happy or not to be away from Cassie's stare. As Brock moved carefully down the steps, his brothers Jose and Diego stepped out of their black truck.

"Hey, Broccoli," Jose said, giving Brock a big trademark grin.

Brock rolled his eyes at the dumb nickname and hugged each of the identical men. "Glad you two could make it. How's the business going?"

Diego just shrugged, but Jose slapped Brock on the back, making pain flare through his body for a moment. Jose didn't notice. "Couldn't be better. We'll be millionaires by the time we're thirty. Soon you'll be part of the family we've forgotten during our rise to fame and fortune."

Jose had always been the joker of the family, and most people were only able to tell him and Diego apart because Jose was the one who always had a smart-ass comment and a wide grin. Diego, the more serious of the two, got down to business. "You've got some fields for us to check out?"

Brock beckoned them to follow, and he walked back into Cassie's home with the two trailing him. "Is your back giving you trouble again?" Diego asked, more aware than his twin, as usual.

Brock nodded. "I fell just a couple of minutes ago. Should be fine soon enough."

He brought Jose and Diego into the kitchen. He could see Cassie from the window, dragging the boards back into a pile. He should've known she wouldn't waste any time waiting for him, though he wasn't sure how much he'd be able to do with his back the way it was.

He turned back to the kitchen, about to tell his brothers to follow him outside, only to find a strange sight behind him: Zach and Carter, standing side-by-side, staring up at Jose and Diego. The two pairs of twins gave each other a once-over. A twice-over? Brock didn't think that was a thing, but it definitely applied to this moment.

"You look the same," Zach commented.

Jose and Diego glanced at each other. "So do you," Diego said.

Zach and Carter shook their heads in unison. "Nuh-uh," Carter said.

"Carter has more freckles on his nose," Zach added.

"And Zach's eyes are darker," Carter finished.

Jose and Diego nodded, as if this made perfect sense. "Diego has a scar next to his ear," Jose said.

"And Jose is more obnoxious," Diego said.

Jose smiled. "Very true."

Zach and Carter seemed to accept all this. They ran out the back door together.

Jose and Diego turned back to Brock, who'd watched the proceedings with enjoyment.

"Hay?" Diego prompted.

Brock nodded and they went through the back door as well, shielding their eyes from the afternoon sunlight. Cassie looked up from the two young boys, who seemed to be in the middle of a long and hurried story, and Brock's heart jumped at the sight of her. If she wasn't just so damned beautiful…

Jose walked up to her, hand outstretched. "Hello. I'm Brock's much more attractive and successful younger brother."

Jose gave Brock a wink as he shook hands with Cassie. Normally, Brock would wink back, or at least roll his eyes at his brother's antics, but this time was different, and the best he could do was try not to scowl at him. What did Jose think he was playing at? He was here to check out some hay, *not* the owner.

Diego walked up and gave Cassie a quick handshake before starting in on questions about the acreage of crops she had to sell. Brock always thought Diego was the smarter of the two.

Before Cassie could answer, Carter tugged on her shirt. "Momma! What about the splinters?"

Cassie leaned down to him. "If you couldn't find the tweezers, they must still be in a box somewhere. Once I finish what I'm doing, I'll go help you search, and then we'll be able to get out all the splinters."

"Do you have a bad one? I can get it out using a credit card," Brock offered.

Cassie gave him a skeptical look. "You can get splinters out using a credit card?"

Brock smiled, carefully extricated his wallet from his back pocket and pulled out a credit card. "Sure. They didn't teach you that in your big-city college?" he asked, glad to clear the air from their earlier heated moment.

"I must've missed that day," she said. "Carter, do you want to show Brock your splinter?"

Brock took the young boy's hand in his, stretching the skin around the splinter. In a few moments, he had used the corner of the card to push the splinter out.

"Cool!" Carter exclaimed, his eyes wide.

Brock looked up to Cassie, who nodded in agreement. "That *was* pretty cool. I'll need to remember that trick."

Diego cleared his throat, bringing Brock out of the moment. "I'll keep an eye on the boys. You three go talk business," he said.

Soon, Cassie was walking with Jose and Diego out into the fields and Brock was directing the boys on the final additions to the lumber pile while he stretched his back. If he could loosen it up some, he and Cassie would be able to get her doctor's office all ready before he needed to leave for the evening. Amy had flown in that morning and, with Jose and Diego now in town, he'd be expected at the family dinner Ma had mentioned.

Brock reached toward his toes as far as he could until the scream of pain quieted. When he straightened, his eyes sought out Cassie and his brothers, who had moved a good distance away, and he could only see the backs of their heads as they talked and gestured. He tried not to imagine Cassie laughing at Jose's jokes, smiling back at him when he gave her his patented thousand-watt grin.

Brock kept stretching, getting more and more annoyed at the efforts he was sure Jose was putting into seducing Cassie. Luckily, they were back before Brock's imagination could run away with him too much, and Jose and Diego shook Cassie's hand once more. Jose said, "It was so nice to meet you, Cass. Everything will be baled and out of your hair by the end of next week. And please think about the dinner invitation, okay?"

Cassie nodded and smiled back, but before she could say anything more to Jose, Brock broke in. "I'll see you two out."

With that he stomped toward the side of the house, knowing the two would need to follow before Jose could say anything else. In a flash and despite the still-prominent ache in his back, he had made his way through a broken section of fence and around the side of the house, until he could see his brothers' truck waiting beside his in the driveway.

"Whoa, what's the rush?" Jose asked as Brock ushered them toward the vehicle.

Brock thought he might hit his brother, but Diego got there first, smacking Jose on the back of the head. "You're lucky Brock's not killing you right now," he said.

"What? Why?" Jose asked, rubbing the back of his head.

"Cass? Dinner? What's with the smooth talk, Jose?" Brock said, folding his arms in front of him.

"I was just being polite," Jose said in his defense.

"You were being fresh," Brock shot back.

Diego jumped in. "Brock, nobody says 'fresh.' Stop acting like an old man. Jose, brothers don't go after the same girls. Brock was here first, and if he has a thing going with Cassie—"

"I don't have a *thing* with her," denied Brock. "It's just that…" He searched for an explanation that didn't involve the story of how she'd shot him down when he asked her out. "She's our parents' new neighbor, and a very nice widow, and she doesn't need to fend off your flirtations."

Diego raised an eyebrow. "Nothing's going on with you two? Seriously?"

Brock wasn't sure what to say to that. "We're friends" sounded like a lie, but what else were they? If he was being honest with himself, he had no answer. No answer he liked, anyway.

The silence lengthened between them until Jose burst out, "Fine, I will no longer be, um, *polite* to Cass.

I mean, Mrs. Stanford," he added after seeing the look on Brock's face.

Brock nodded and walked them the last few steps to their truck.

"In my defense, though," Jose continued, "I wasn't asking her *out* to dinner. I was inviting her to dinner at home. Ma told me to. So don't worry so much about me getting too fresh, Grandpa."

With that and another big smile, Jose hopped into the passenger side of the truck. Diego shook his head. "I'll keep him under control. See you in a few hours?"

Brock nodded and Diego got into the driver's seat and started the engine. Brock turned around, feeling equal parts annoyed and ashamed.

He had jumped down his brother's throat for flirting with Cassie. If they were just going to be friends, why should he get to say who flirted with her? Brock knew that wasn't fair to her, or to Jose, or to any guy who liked her. If she didn't want to date because of her husband's memory, that was fine, but he should leave that decision to her. She could decide to go out with anybody she liked.

Still, the thought of Cassie with someone else bothered him more than he wanted to admit.

Brock ran his fingers through his hair. If he could survive another ten days around her, it wouldn't matter, anyway. He'd go back to his regular life and that would be it for this whole thing.

Brock sighed and went back to where Cassie was standing, the pile of boards back to the state it had been before it tumbled. The boys were nowhere to be seen.

Her eyes lit up when she saw him in a way he was sure Jose would never experience, and in that moment of triumph, he threw caution to the wind and kissed her again, hoping that this time...

Any thought after that disappeared as her body and lips met his, sending bursts of electricity flowing through his veins. He wrapped his arms around her and held her close, though she needed no urging.

Then she pulled away, and in a flash his arms were empty and she was standing beside the dilapidated fence, not looking at him and shaking her head.

Brock laughed ruefully. "If that kiss did anything near to you what it did to me, then your husband must've been some amazing guy for you to be so loyal to him."

It was Cassie's turn to laugh, though hers was bitter and hinted at struggles beyond her young years. "Hank? If he'd survived the car crash, we would be divorced and I would probably still be kissing you right now. He was...not a very good husband."

Brock was confused. Everything he'd heard about the man painted him as a saint. Cassie seemed to know what he was thinking. "I don't want the boys to know the darker sides of their father. For now at least, they should think of him as a heroic police officer."

"Instead of..." Brock prompted.

He could see the pain in her eyes, and thought she might want to share the story. When she didn't speak at first, though, he opened his mouth to change the subject. Before he could say anything she began speaking, all in a rush, as if the words had been walled up and the dam had just burst.

"Hank was a cop back in Minneapolis. I got pregnant when we had only been dating for a few months, and we got married. Things started to fall apart even before the boys were born, and we had a lot of arguments about me going back to school to finish getting my MD. Still, I tried to stick it out."

Brock watched her intently. Cassie took a deep breath and continued. "He was gone a lot—working extra shifts, he said—which meant we didn't see much of each other those last couple of years. It was probably the reason we stayed together as long as we did. But—"

She paused. Brock wasn't sure she was going to continue. When she spoke again, her voice was quiet.

"But I had no idea what was really going on. It was only after the accident that I found out. He got in a car crash in the middle of the night. He'd crashed into a pole. He died…"

She grimaced, either in hurt or disgust, Brock wasn't sure. "The woman in the passenger seat survived."

Brock moved forward and stood beside her, aching with the betrayal she must have felt. "She was—"

"His girlfriend," Cassie said, the calmness of her voice belied by the sparkle of a tear in her eye. "One of many, it turned out."

Brock wasn't sure what to say, but before he could find words, Cassie continued, "And they found drugs in the car, too. I had been so busy with the twins and finishing my residency that I had no idea any of this was going on. I felt so stupid."

Cassie covered her face with her hands and fell silent for a moment. Brock wanted to hug her, but held himself back, only looping a single arm around her back as a show of support. She dropped her hands back to her side and forced herself to continue.

"The rumors about Hank were everywhere. He was a cop, after all. A 'pillar of the community' sort of thing. Every person we talked to would look at us with pity, and I hated it. I didn't want the scandal of it to ruin the boys' memories of their dad. So I packed them up and moved them across the country to keep them safe and happy. Sometimes I'm not so sure it was a great idea, but here we are," she said, standing and looking out the barn toward the ranch house.

"Anyway, that's why nothing can happen between us. I'm not loyal to Hank's memory. I'm loyal to Zach and Carter and the memories of their father that they hold so dear. They've been through so much, and we're finally getting into a good place. I don't want to do *anything* to jeopardize that. That means no dating, no kissing, no flings, regardless of the man."

Brock could see in her face and hear in her voice how much she desired him, and if it didn't give him what he really wanted, at least it soothed the feeling of rejection. Before he could do more than nod, the twins came running up to their mom, chattering excitedly about their adventures searching for the tool chest.

Cassie looked up at Brock, none of the emotions she had experienced so recently showing on her face. "I sent Zach and Carter to find the toolbox so we can work on the office, unless you need to get home and be with your family?" she asked.

She was giving him an out, a chance to slink away

without discussing all that had happened in the past few minutes. He knew she would understand if he walked away now and never came back. "I've got enough time to help. And if we have that out of the way, we can get started on the paddock tomorrow."

Cassie's smile transmitted her relief without the need for words, and Brock walked with her and the boys into the house. He wished there was something he could do to convince her that she deserved to be happy as much as her children did.

But if he couldn't do that, at least he could respect her wishes and do whatever possible to make her life a little easier. If anyone deserved a helping hand, it was Cassie.

AN HOUR AND a half later, Cassie watched from her doorway as Brock walked to his parents' house. She wasn't sure if she was relieved or disappointed that they'd never had a chance to speak privately after her confession by the fence. The boys had been so eager to help as they hung her diplomas and organized the furniture, there was no opportunity for her and Brock to be alone.

So Cassie couldn't help but wonder what he thought about everything she'd said. It was clear Brock was still willing to help her, but that was all she knew.

Once he was out of sight, Cassie walked into the kitchen and took a long drink of cold water. She had just put the glass down and started to consider what to do with the rest of the afternoon when her phone buzzed. She glanced at it to find a message from Brock: Ma wanted me to make sure you were coming to dinner. Will you be coming? She wants you here by 6.

Dinner with the McNeals. An entire night of unsatisfied lust for Brock and fending off Jose's flirtations didn't sound all that appealing, but she couldn't find it in her to say no. Mrs. McNeal was so nice, after all, and she didn't want to disappoint the old woman.

Cassie knew it was a lie to say she was going for any reason besides Brock. She might not be able to have him, but she still couldn't stop herself from spending what time around him she could. Even when she engineered ways to stay away from him, she still managed to sabotage them.

She cut off the internal monologue and texted back. We'll be there.

Once the decision was made, Cassie went to tell Zach and Carter. Then they needed to decide what to bring their hosts, and she would need to go through the long process of agonizing over what to wear so it wasn't flirtatious, yet attractive enough that the little voice inside her still hoping for some impossible romance didn't shout too loudly.

A quick trip to the bakery solved one of her problems, and an hour in front of the mirror solved the other, and by that time it was nearly six o'clock and she had to hustle Zach and Carter out the door.

Cassie watched her boys run ahead of her through the late-afternoon sunshine toward the McNeal home. The lights shone through the windows, creating an inviting scene, but it did nothing to ease Cassie's nerves. She told herself that she was just nervous because she was planning to spend the evening with a bunch of people she hardly knew, not because of anything to do with Brock McNeal.

She didn't believe it, but it was better than admitting the alternative: that her feelings toward Brock were getting more confusing all the time. She couldn't forget the way her body reacted to his kisses, or the way her heart melted at his smile.

All Cassie wanted to do was get her ranch finished and keep her heart unscathed, and instead she was planning to spend an entire evening in Brock's presence under the eyes of his whole family, who also happened to be her neighbors in her new hometown. She really had a knack for creating the perfect recipe for disaster.

Zach and Carter hopped onto the porch, then waited for their mother to catch up. For one crazy second, Cassie considered calling them back to her and turning around. They could just go home and send their apologies.

The door opened and Mrs. McNeal, an older woman with a head of white curls and a wide smile, greeted the two boys. "Come in! My, but it's good to see young boys in my home again. If I'm not mistaken, you've grown taller since you moved here. 'Fore I know it, you'll be as tall as my boy Brock."

Cassie walked up the porch steps and saw the look of astonishment on the boys' faces. "I'm going to be *that* tall?" Carter asked with wide eyes.

Mrs. McNeal nodded confidently. "Taller, if I'm not mistaken. And I'm never mistaken. Now come in off the porch, you three."

"Thank you for inviting us, Mrs. McNeal," Cassie said as she entered the large, well-kept ranch home.

Brock's mother waved her hands as if getting rid of a bad smell. "Sarah, if you please. We're neighbors, after all. We don't put on any airs here, Cassie."

Before Cassie could reply, Sarah had her arms wrapped around the boys and was leading them through the house. "You two will call me Nana Sarah, won't you? My children haven't given me any grandbabies to spoil yet, so I'll need to spoil you instead."

Cassie followed Sarah and the boys, trying to gird herself for the jolt of electricity she felt every time she saw Brock. Even so, there was no way she could have been prepared for the wash of emotions she felt when she walked into the kitchen, where Brock stood with his arm around the waist of a beautiful, tall blonde woman.

Cassie couldn't believe what she was seeing. Did Brock have a girlfriend he'd never told her about? The pain she'd felt when she discovered the truth about her husband came washing back over her, taking her breath away. Was Brock taken and simply trying to have some extra fun on the side with her? Cassie's heart ached at the thought.

Brock turned toward her, giving her a smile that cut right through her. It hurt to realize that she wasn't as special to him as she'd believed, that he was another cheating man like Hank. She considered running out the door right then and there, but she stopped herself. She wouldn't let another man embarrass her like that.

Chapter Nine

Brock felt his heart speed up at the sight of Cassie standing in the doorway, holding what looked to be another of Emma's pies, which his ma smelled with glee. When Brock smiled at Cassie, though, he was surprised to see her give him a stony expression. He wondered if something had changed since he'd seen her a few hours before. Maybe she was mad about the kiss and regretted telling him about her husband. Or maybe, despite her determination to stay single, she had fallen for Jose's smooth talk after all and had decided to create a cool distance between them before pursuing something with his little brother.

He knew that didn't make sense, but even so, it was difficult to push the thought away.

"Brock, why don't you introduce Cassie to everyone while I take this pie and the boys into the kitchen? I need a couple of taste-testers to help make sure everything's ready," his ma urged, breaking the silence before disappearing through the doorway to the kitchen, boys in tow.

"I know everyone except—" Cassie paused, looking at Amy.

Brock used the arm around Amy's waist to turn her toward Cassie. He tried to grin at her again, hoping he was just reading too much into things. "Cassie, this is Amy, my sister."

"Oh!" Cassie exclaimed, her eyes wide in surprise and maybe something else. Relief?

Cassie shook hands with Amy, her friendly manner completely restored. Brock decided he must have just imagined her previous hesitation. He guided Amy to a chair, where she sat down with a sigh.

"Sorry," Amy said to Cassie's questioning gaze. "I rolled my ankle getting out of the truck earlier today, and it's pretty painful. I'll need to get it checked tomorrow. I can't even make it to the dinner table without help, but I guess that's what big brothers are for," she finished with a wave in Brock's direction.

Jose, who had been lounging against the wall on the other side of the dining room, spoke up. "Amy can climb Mount Fuji without a problem, but getting out of a truck in Spring Valley is apparently a little more than she can handle."

Cassie didn't seem to notice Jose—she was too busy staring at Amy's ankle in concern. It made Brock happy to see how little attention she gave Jose. Even though he knew she wasn't planning on dating anyone, it was still nice to be sure he wouldn't need to watch Jose and Cassie become an item.

"Cassie, would you be willing to take a look at it?" Brock asked, sure that her fingers were itching to help.

It was just the kind of person Cassie was.

She nodded and knelt by Amy's foot. "Do you mind? I'm a doctor."

"You're a *doctor*?" Jose said, clearly surprised.

Brock knew what his brother was thinking: What was a doctor doing buying a ranch in a tiny place like this?

He felt a touch of pride for Cassie and the good work she planned to do in the little town she had decided to call home. "She's turning the old library in the Wilson place into a doctor's office. We'll have a genuine doctor in town, so people won't need to go all the way to the hospital."

Brock's siblings all nodded, clearly seeing the advantages of having Cassie move in. The closest hospital was in the next town over, a pretty long drive. They'd all experienced that interminable trip as children with ear infections or when a cut was so deep that it warranted stitches.

"It'll just be for checkups and minor injuries. Big problems will still need to be examined at the hospital," Cassie amended in her casual, humble way that Brock had grown to love. Like.

As friends.

"Spring Valley will be lucky to have a doctor," Brock told her.

Any town would be lucky to have her, he added silently, glad Cassie couldn't read his thoughts.

She continued to assess Amy's ankle, but he saw a light flush creep up her neck and hoped his affection for her hadn't been blatant. Since her confession, he had resolved to put a little distance between them, both physically and metaphorically, and already it was a difficult promise to keep.

Cassie seemed willing to let the moment pass, though, so he said nothing more. She looked up from Amy's ankle, but kept her eyes on his sister and didn't look Brock's way, for which he was grateful. He was pretty sure any eye contact between them would be send a clear signal about his feelings to his hawk-eyed family.

He couldn't say what it was, but being with her around his family changed things, somehow. Watching her help Amy, greet his mother with a pie. She just fit.

He took a small step back, as if hoping he could force himself to fade into the background.

"It doesn't seem to be broken," she said at last. "But it's a pretty bad sprain. I'd like to wrap it and put some ice on it to reduce swelling."

"Beautiful *and* smart? I may have stayed in Spring Valley if I'd known someone like you would turn up," Jose commented from his corner.

Before Brock could do more than glare at his brother, Diego stood up. "I'll go find the first-aid kit for you," he said to Cassie, heading toward the kitchen. "Jose, you come help me."

Jose slunk over to his twin and followed him into the next room. Brock was sure Diego was going to give Jose a quick reminder to back off, and he couldn't pretend to be displeased.

Cassie nodded her thanks to them, then turned back to Amy. "Keep it elevated as much as you can for the next couple of days. I'll check it again in a day or two to make sure it's healing, if that's okay with you."

Amy nodded. "Thanks. Hopefully it'll be fine by Tuesday. That's when I'm flying out."

As if on cue, Ma walked into the room, her hands on her hips. "Why you need to leave so soon is beyond me, Amy dear. You just got home."

Amy shrugged. "Sorry, Ma. I need to be in Marrakech by Wednesday."

Ma harrumphed and walked back into the kitchen, passing a confused Diego as he returned with the kit. Cassie began rummaging around for the necessary bandage while Jose gave her a bag of ice, very clearly avoiding making eye contact with her.

Amy turned back to Cassie. "Sorry about that. Families, you know. And thanks for looking at my ankle."

Cassie finished wrapping Amy's ankle with practiced hands and stood. "Any time. I owe your family a pretty large debt, what with Brock helping me fix up the place and Jose and Diego agreeing to buy my bales of hay. Your ankle balances out the scales a little."

Before anyone could say another word, Zach and Carter walked into the room carrying plates and silverware. "Nana Sarah said for you lazybones to get to work like us," Carter announced, dropping a handful of cutlery onto the table with a clatter.

"Carter!" Cassie admonished, shaking her head disapprovingly.

Brock tried to hold in the laughter at the look of surprise on Carter's face. The kid clearly had no idea why his mom was so shocked at him.

Ma peeked her head into the room. "Did you call them lazybones like I said?" she asked Carter.

"Yes, Nana Sarah," Carter said, still looking slightly distressed.

Ma nodded approvingly. "Well that's all right, then. And you—" she said, pointing at Brock accusingly. "Stop your snorting over there and get to work. You heard the boy."

"Yes, Ma," Brock answered, grinning widely.

Sarah McNeal didn't pull any punches, that was for sure. He glanced over at Cassie. She turned to him and their eyes met. He shrugged, hoping she would be understanding about his slightly eccentric mother. Cassie laughed. "Get to work, lazybones," she told him.

Without thinking, Brock laughed, too, threw his arm around her shoulders and kissed her playfully on the cheek.

Brock wasn't sure if the rest of the house suddenly got silent, or if it was just that he had stopped caring about anything else going on. Cassie looked up at him, and for a second he was sure she was going to lean in and kiss him. His heart stuttered.

Then she looked away. "I'll go get napkins," she said, and without another glance in his direction, she walked into the kitchen.

"Smooth," Amy said, rolling her eyes.

Jose started setting the table. "Oh, like you're so great at love, Ames. How many years has it been since the last time you were with a guy?"

"That wasn't cool, Jose," Amy responded, turning red from either anger or embarrassment.

Brock left the room, ignoring the argument starting between his siblings. Why couldn't he control himself around Cassie? He knew she was determined to avoid even so much as a brief relationship, and yet he still found he was unable to stop himself.

The living room was much quieter, which suited him just fine. He needed time to think. He sat down on the old couch, an ugly patterned thing that must have dated from the sixties. The springs creaked as they took his weight.

Brock battled with his frustration. There was only one thing he could do, it seemed, to be sure he didn't attempt to kiss Cassie again: no more trying to be friends. And no more close encounters. He'd go over to her place and work as far away from her as he could.

He wished there was some other way, because he truly enjoyed spending time with her, but it didn't seem like he had any other option.

That shock of electricity, the pure joy of the moment, didn't feel like a light, casual nothing to him. It felt like a big, definite, something. It wasn't a passionate kiss full of lust like the others. It was…sweet. And loving. And that broke all his rules, too.

Brock sighed and put his head in his hands, wishing things could be different.

After a few seconds of silence, Brock felt a small tap on his shoulder and looked up. Zach was standing there staring at him. He looked nervous.

Brock knew just what had the boy so worried, and couldn't help but smile despite his other thoughts. "What did Nana Sarah call me?"

"A laggard."

"All right, I'm coming," Brock said as he stood up, resolving to act natural when he saw Cassie.

"Brock, what's a laggard?" Zach asked, almost in a whisper. "Is it a bad word?"

Brock chuckled at the concern in Zach's voice. "It's just another word for lazy."

Zach looked visibly relieved as he ran back to the kitchen shouting, "Nana Sarah! I told him just like you said!"

Back in the dining room, platters of food covered the large table. His ma had apparently made enough to feed a small army. "You might've outdone yourself this time, Ma," he said as he surveyed the steaming chicken fried steak and pile of mashed potatoes.

Sarah looked at the spread with pride. "I wanted our new neighbors to have some good ol' Southern food. Everybody sit down and tuck in while it's hot."

Brock took his usual seat, only to find Cassie seated next to him. A glance at Ma's face was enough to tell him she had orchestrated the seating arrangements. Brock decided to enjoy these last few minutes this close to her.

"Your ma sure knows how to cook," Cassie said, though the way she kept her eyes trained away from him belied her relaxed tone.

Brock nodded, unable to bring himself to share in much conversation. As he bit a green bean in half, Amy caught his eye. She was clearly still sore about Jose's comment, but she raised her eyebrows at him, silently asking if he was okay. Brock gave her a little nod, though he wasn't sure if that was the truth.

CASSIE WAS GLAD the food in front of her gave her a reason not to look at Brock, since she wasn't sure she could do so without making a simpering fool of herself. That kiss on the cheek, though so much tamer than the other kisses they had shared, made her melt in an entirely different way. It was…sweet.

That scared her.

So she kept her head down and ate, glad that the silence of everyone tucking in meant she didn't need to try to make conversation. And that lasted a short while, at least.

"Cass—Dr. Stanford," Jose said, in a formal way that struck her as odd. "How are you settling in?"

Everyone's eyes turned to her as they waited for her answer.

Cassie swallowed and answered honestly, "This town already feels like home."

She didn't mention how much Brock's help had been a part of that.

"So you're adjusting to small-town life okay? You don't wish you were working in a big hospital?" Diego asked.

Cassie nodded, thinking of her horses and ranch, and of the cowboy who had become a part of all that so quickly. Small-town life suited her just fine. "I love my little office," she said. "And I'm going to see my first patient tomorrow morning, actually. This is the kind of doctor I always wanted to be."

"I bet Brock can't wait to be examined by you," Jose said quietly, but not quietly enough.

Diego smacked him on the head, and Howard said a warning, *"Jose!"* from the other side of the table.

All at once, Jose calling her Dr. Stanford instead of "Cass" made sense. Brock must have told his brother something about what had happened between them, probably to get Jose to back off. Why else would Jose change his behavior toward her so quickly?

And judging by everyone's reaction, he'd told them, too. They all seemed to believe she and Brock were some kind of an item.

What had he told them, exactly? Did they know about the kisses? About Hank?

A picture of the whole family sitting around dissecting everything she'd said and done with Brock made her stomach churn. And what if it all got around town, twisting and morphing until she couldn't show her face in Spring Valley?

It was Minneapolis all over again.

"How about we have some pie?" Sarah said, standing from her place at the table.

Cassie felt claustrophobic. She needed to get out of there. She stood as well, grasping for some excuse to leave. "Actually, we need to leave," she said, hoping she sounded calm. "I didn't realize how late it was, and Zach and Carter need to go to bed."

The boys looked up, distressed. "We don't get dessert?" Carter asked.

"Diego was going to let me wear his cowboy hat after dinner," Zach added.

Cassie was in no mood to stick around. "Not this

time. Go get your shoes on," she told them, and the two boys left the table without another word.

Before Cassie could rush her children out the door, Brock appeared. He was the last person she wanted to see.

"I'll walk you home," Brock offered.

"No," Cassie almost shouted before regaining control of herself. "We can manage, thanks."

As Cassie opened the door to let herself out, Sarah came running in from the dining room, a plate of pie in her hands. "I'll be darned if I'm going to let my unruly children eat all the delicious pie you brought over without your sweethearts getting some," she insisted, shoving the plate into Cassie's hands.

Cassie hardly had the sense of mind to thank the older woman before she was out the door, her two boys hurrying to keep up. She wanted to get away from there as fast as she could. Before she could leave the pool of light created by the ranch house's windows, though, she heard Brock rushing up behind her. "Cassie, wait."

She turned toward him, her irritation boiling inside her.

"Jose—" he started.

She cut him off before he could say another word. "I don't want to talk about this. I just…" She trailed off.

I just thought you were different, she wanted to say, but she could feel tears of frustration welling in her eyes. She turned and continued on her way home before she could let them fall.

It was only after Cassie had given Zach and Carter their pie and tucked them into bed—then taken a long bath to try to soothe her muscles and thoughts—that she glanced at her phone as she placed it on her bedside table.

A few minutes after she'd left the McNeal house hours before, Brock had sent her a text. Jose was making a joke at my expense. Because it's obvious to everyone who knows me how much I like you. I set them all straight and they hope you aren't too mad. I'm sorry.

Cassie understood her mistake immediately and looked out her window, which faced the McNeal house. The entire place was dark. It was too late to go talk to Brock.

He hadn't told them anything about her, obviously. Since when had she gotten so suspicious of other people, so ready to see the worst in men?

She knew the answer to that, of course. Since the day she'd learned about Hank's affairs.

Cassie resolved to go see Brock right after her morning appointment. She needed to apologize, and it needed to be in person. He deserved that much.

She turned off the light, even though she knew it would be a long time until she'd be able to fall asleep. She had a lot to think over.

She awoke the next morning to her alarm beeping at her, and opened her bleary eyes to the sun streaming in through the window. It looked to be another bright, hot day, though at this point in the summer, that came as no surprise.

Cassie turned off the alarm, thankful she'd set one

to be sure she didn't sleep too late. She'd had a nearly sleepless night, and would likely have slept until noon if she could.

Then her two human alarm clocks came running in, reminding her that it'd be a long time until she'd be able to sleep until noon, regardless of appointments with patients.

"Momma!" Carter called as he and Zach pounced on her. "Are we going to paint our room today?"

Cassie grimaced. The prospect of painting alone was unpleasant, but she'd need to apologize before she could even think about asking Brock to do more work on her house. "Maybe later, honey," she said. "I have a patient coming this morning, remember? And Brock might not be coming over today."

Zach looked worried. "Why isn't Brock coming today? Is it because I called him a laggard? Nana Sarah told me to!"

Cassie's heart ached at the distress on his face. She gathered her sons into a tight hug. "Brock isn't mad at you, I promise. You did nothing wrong. I just haven't asked him if he'll be around today, yet. I'll do that right after the appointment"

And eat a little crow, she added silently.

Cassie rose and dressed quickly, throwing a doctor's smock on over scrubs, and while the boys ate breakfast, she went into her office for one final check before her first patient arrived.

She put the last item into place none too soon, because the doorbell rang as she closed the cupboard. With one last backward glance, Cassie rushed to the door and opened it to find Emma and a friendly-look-ing old woman on the other side.

Emma gave Cassie a broad smile. "Mrs. Edelman, meet the town's new resident doctor. Dr. Stanford."

Despite everything going on with Brock, Cassie's mood lifted. She'd missed being a doctor and was ex-cited to meet her first patient. The older woman gave her a strong handshake and a huge smile. In her thick Texas drawl, she said, "Oh, dear, am I ever glad to meet you. Spring Valley has needed a doctor. You, honey, are a godsend."

Cassie blushed. "I'm happy to be of help. Would you like to come into my examination room?" she asked, gesturing Mrs. Edelman through the door to the library-turned-office.

"I have a couple of cuties to feed and entertain," Emma said, holding up a bag that clearly held treats from her bakery. "You two holler if you need me."

With that, Emma was gone and her neighbor was settling herself onto the examination table. "What can I help you with today, Mrs. Edelman?" Cassie asked, realizing that in all the rush to get everything ready in time, she'd never asked what exactly her patient wanted to see her about.

The older woman's grin grew even wider, if that were possible. "I need vaccinations. I'll be leaving to see the world, and it wouldn't do to die of malaria as soon as I leave. This is my itinerary," she said, hand-ing Cassie a couple of folded sheets filled with travel details.

Cassie read through the list of cities, amazed at the

variety. It seemed Mrs. Edelman was planning a round-the-world trip that any twenty-year-old nomad would be proud of. "You are quite the adventurer," she commented.

"Oh, my dear, I've never been outside of Texas. I've wanted to see the world my entire life, and now I'm going to do it, come hell or high water," she said, the ferocity in her voice surprising.

"I don't doubt you will," Cassie said. "I'll need to go through this list of places and see what vaccinations you should get, and then I'll order them. Would you mind coming back for another visit before you leave so I can administer them?"

Mrs. Edelman nodded. "That would be perfectly lovely."

"Since you're already here, would you like to have a quick checkup to make sure you're ready to trek across the globe?" Cassie asked, pulling out a pair of gloves.

"So long as you don't tell me I should stay home, poke and prod away," the older woman responded.

Cassie smiled as she pulled out a blood pressure cuff. "I wouldn't dream of doing that. You seem so determined that I doubt it would do any good if I did, anyway."

"Well," Mrs. Edelman said, looking at Cassie thoughtfully, "I should have gone long ago, but I was too busy being a wife and a mother to do what I wanted for myself. If I could go back and change things, I would. I'd have lovely memories of the pyramids and the Taj Mahal, and what's the worst that could've happened? Fred and the kids might've needed to cook a dinner or two. It would have done us all some good if I was a bit more selfish back then. But it's too late to change that now, so I'll just need to start from here and see what I can while I have any juice left in this old body of mine."

Cassie shook her head in amazement at her first patient and completed a careful examination, happy to declare that the woman seemed to be in fine health. Mrs. Edelman gathered her purse and scooted off the table. Cassie showed her into the living room as she went in search of the old woman's ride home, the idea that had been formulating since her conversation with Mrs. Edelman still in the forefront of her mind.

When she saw Emma playing trucks with the boys, she came to a decision. "Emma, Mrs. Edelman is ready whenever you are."

Emma stood up, stretched, and went to her friend. "Your boys are wonderful, Cassie."

"I'm glad you think so, because I have a favor to ask," Cassie said. "Would you take them with you and watch them for a couple of hours? I need them out of the house for a bit."

Cassie expected her nosy friend to ask what she had planned, but luckily Emma just nodded. "No problem! I don't need to be at the bakery until two this afternoon. Is it okay if I bring them back about an hour before that?"

Cassie agreed, relieved. "That's perfect. Thanks. I owe you one."

Emma pulled up her sleeve to reveal the nearly healed scar from her burn. "Already paid in full. Come on, boys! Your momma says I get to take you home and feed you more delicious sweets!"

The boys jumped up, excited. Emma turned to Cassie, noting the slight frown on her face. "Hey, if you don't want them eating dessert for lunch, don't let a baker babysit."

With that and a laugh, the four of them left the room, and a few minutes later, Cassie was waving goodbye as they disappeared into the distance. As soon as the car was out of sight, she turned back to the house, intending to change out of her scrubs quickly before heading over to Brock's.

Before she could put a foot onto the porch, however, Cassie paused and listened. It took her a few seconds to realize that what she was hearing was hammering, and it seemed to be coming from behind her house.

Curious, Cassie followed the noise to find Brock working on her paddock, nailing a new piece of lumber into place. Based on the pile of lumber beside him, he'd been at it for quite a while despite how early it was.

Cassie walked up to Brock without him noticing, and when he stopped to examine the board he'd just nailed in place, she said, "Decided to get an early start, huh?"

He jumped slightly and turned to her, giving her a grin that made her weak at the knees. He shrugged. "Yeah, well, I figured I had a readymade metaphor here, so I came over to mend some fences. Metaphorically and—" he gestured at the paddock "—literally."

Cassie smiled at the terrible pun. "I'm sorry I overreacted last night. I'm still not quite over what happened in Minneapolis, and I let it get to my head," she told him.

Her heart pounded as she gathered her courage.

Brock shook his head. "You don't need to apologize—"

Before he could say another word, Cassie pulled him into a kiss.

Brock seemed stunned for a moment, but then his arms wrapped around her and he kissed her back enthusiastically. After a long, long kiss that neither of them seemed willing to break, they finally came up for air. Brock gave Cassie a pained smile and pressed his forehead against hers. "It seems we're both terrible at controlling ourselves, huh?" he asked.

Cassie shook her head, and moved even closer to him. "I'm done controlling myself," she said.

Brock moved back just enough to look her straight in the eyes, a surprised look on her face.

"I got some good advice today. If I wait until the boys are grown to do anything for myself, it might be too late, and I don't want that. It won't hurt them if I'm a little selfish and impulsive for the next nine days."

"Nine days," Brock repeated, though Cassie couldn't quite tell what emotion he was feeling when he said it.

She nodded resolutely, as much for herself as for him. "Until the rodeo. We can work on the house, and in the small snatches of time when the boys aren't around, we can do...more grown-up activities."

Brock smiled. "We better make them a good nine days," he commented.

Cassie kept talking, anxiety building now that she

knew what might come next. "Plus, I need some help if I'm ever going to get over what happened with Hank. It affected me more than I realized. I need to practice being in a relationship again, even if it's only a short one."

"So I'm your training wheels?" Brock asked, tipping her head up with a single finger.

"Not exactly," Cassie backpedaled, trying not to blush.

But Brock said nothing, just leaned in for another kiss.

Chapter Ten

When they separated this time, Brock could hardly think straight. That morning he had woken up expecting little more than to hopefully smooth things out with Cassie and continue working on her ranch while also staying as far from her as possible. Now he was kissing her, touching her, and had even more to look forward to in the future.

Well, for the next nine days.

He didn't want to waste any of it. "Where are Zach and Carter?" he asked.

"Emma's watching them," Cassie said, still breathless. "She's bringing them back around one."

Plenty of time. On to the next important question. "Have you eaten yet today?"

"No," she answered. "I didn't have time before—where are we going?" she asked as he grabbed her hand and began pulling her away from the paddock.

"We need breakfast," he replied, not slowing down. "We're going on a date!"

"Oh!" Cassie exclaimed, and Brock paused and looked back at her.

In the rush to get the most out of every second, he

was getting ahead of himself. "Do you want to go on a breakfast date with me?"

"Absolutely," she answered, so emphatically that it made him grin. Or maybe a grin was just permanently plastered on his face after what had happened during the past ten minutes. "I just thought we'd be..."

She looked at the house, and when he realized what she'd been thinking, he needed to take a deep breath to calm himself down. As much as he wanted to, that wasn't how he did things. "You deserve a delicious breakfast, don't you think?"

"I should just change," she said, waving a hand at her scrub and smock.

Brock didn't think he'd ever seen her in anything so sexy. "If you want to," he said, "but I think you look just perfect."

"Two minutes," she said, running into the house.

Brock paced in front of his truck, which was still parked beside her house, his stomach in knots. He was going on a date with Cassie. And after that, well, he could hardly allow his mind to go there.

Cassie came back out of the house all in a rush, slipping low flats onto her feet as she went. She had changed into a knee-length dress that nearly killed him, made of some shiny brown material that set off the fiery accents in her hair.

"It's been a long time since I've been on a date," she said breathlessly once she reached him. "I want to be dressed for it."

He managed to unglue his tongue enough to tell her

how beautiful she was and give her another deep kiss before helping her into his truck.

In moments, they were out of her driveway and heading to his favorite little restaurant. "I hope you don't mind cheesy diners with delicious food," he told her. "It's one of my favorite places, and it's a little ways out of town."

He wasn't sure if she wanted to keep everything, even them going to eat together, a secret, but if she did, this was the best location. People in town usually went to one of the two restaurants on the main drag, not fifteen minutes out into the middle of nowhere.

"Sounds perfect," she answered, and he settled into the drive.

The silence between them felt charged and tense as they went. After a few minutes, Cassie said his name in a serious voice that made him worry she was rethinking her earlier decision.

"You should know, before we go any further," she started.

He waited for the bomb to drop.

"I'm a mother first. This can be a fun thing, but we need to keep it from affecting my kids in any way," Cassie finished.

Brock laughed in relief. There was no new information there. "I'd never do anything to hurt Zach and Carter," he told her truthfully.

Cassie leaned back. "Then let's go have a date," she said.

THE LITTLE RESTAURANT Brock took her to reminded Cassie of diners in movies, complete with a cherry pie under glass and a large pottery cowboy boot painted with desert scenes in dusky reds and yellows. Brock maneuvered her through the place to a small corner booth. "Best spot in the restaurant," he said.

He didn't need to tell her that. It was secluded, almost private, and small enough that they were sitting nearly shoulder-to-shoulder. Her heart raced as he waited for her to sit before seating himself. "You are quite the gentleman on a date," she commented.

He smiled. "My ma raised me right," he said.

Cassie looked through the menu, but the combination of nerves and the variety of options made it difficult to choose. The diner seemed to serve pretty much everything under the sun.

Finally, she settled on the French toast. Brock ordered a corned beef skillet and a side of dumplings.

"Dumplings?" Cassie asked as soon as the waitress was gone.

"Their dumplings are fantastic," Brock answered. "You need to try them. If that means you're eating dumplings before ten, well, then, so be it."

She was skeptical, but said nothing. Brock seemed so happy to be out with her that she couldn't spoil any part of it, even if it involved having a pan-fried treat with her French toast.

Luckily, the meal ended up being fantastic, dumplings and all. Almost as good as the conversation and sexual tension.

By the time they'd finished eating, she wanted nothing more than to take Brock home and fulfill a few of her fantasies. So when they were both in his car and he asked, "Do you want to go see a movie or something?" she put her foot down.

"You're killing me, Brock!" she said, exasperated.

He laughed. "This is how I treat ladies I'm dating," he said. "Would you rather we just go back to your place?"

"Yes!"

"Thank God," he said and turned the truck in the direction of her ranch.

The drive felt far too long for Cassie, and she wished they'd gone to eat somewhere in town, despite the chances of gossip and missing out on amazing dumplings. She could feel the time dwindling away, even though she knew they still had a couple of hours before the boys came home.

Brock seemed to be thinking the same thing, because the moment the truck was parked in front of her home, he leaned over and pulled her into a kiss ripe with urgency, as if every moment counted.

That could've just been desperate need, though. She felt that, too, as all the pent-up desire from the past few days took over, and she nearly crawled into his lap to get closer. The heat of the day quickly warmed the car to an almost unbearable temperature, and finally they broke apart, gasping. They looked one another in the eye, and as if by silent agreement, they opened their doors and rushed for the house.

Inside the dim, cool house, Brock seemed to feel the need to slow things down. After the door closed behind them, he took her in his arms and ran one hand over her face, moving her hair out of her eyes. She nearly melted from his tender touch.

Just as he leaned in toward her with agonizing slowness, the tinkling music of Cassie's phone broke through the moment, making her want to scream with frustration. She briefly considered letting the phone go to voice mail, but reminded herself that it could be Emma or a patient and they came first, and she dug it out of her purse.

"Dr. Stanford speaking," she said, hoping it would be quick.

"Dr. Stanford, my name is Melody. I live in town. Got your card from the bakery."

Cassie could hear a baby wailing in the background. "Hi, Melody. What can I do for you?" she asked, even though she had a guess, based on the strength of the cries.

"It's my daughter, Lizzie. She's sick and won't stop crying. Is there any way you can see her?"

Cassie could hear the worry in the woman's voice— one that sounded quite young. She knew that anything between her and Brock would need to wait. "Bring her over as soon as you can. You still have my card with the address?"

"I do. Thank you, Doctor," Melody replied, and the gratitude in her voice tugged at Cassie's heartstrings.

After Cassie had hung up, she kept looking at her phone. She didn't want to see the disappointment in Brock's face.

"Is there something wrong with Lizzie?" he asked, catching her by surprise.

"How did you know?" she asked.

Brock didn't look disappointed like she'd expected. Only worried. He said, "Melody had a baby girl six months or so ago. My ma says she's a sweet little thing. She's helped Melody out some when she can. Her fiancée up and left when she was a few months pregnant, and she's been working herself to the bone to provide for Lizzie. She's Melody's whole world."

Cassie put her hand on his arm. "I'll do everything I can for her. She'll be here any minute."

Brock nodded. "How about I work on getting Zach and Carter's room ready for painting? If you're still with Lizzie when the boys get here, I'll keep an eye on them. And if you finish up in time…" he said, brushing his lips against hers in a way that both excited and frustrated her.

He seemed to sense her mood and chuckled. "Hey, worst-case scenario, you can always hide me under your bed until the kids are asleep, and I can sneak out the window in the middle of the night. Real clandestine secret-affair type stuff."

She laughed, though she wasn't completely sure he was kidding. The idea didn't sound half-bad, either.

Cassie hardly had time to change into her scrubs before the doorbell rang. By the time she got to the door, Brock was there, holding a screaming baby and talking to the anxious-looking mother. She only caught the end of what he was saying, "—will do everything she can to help."

Melody's forehead smoothed a little at his words, and Cassie put her hand to her heart at the sentiment. She quickly gathered her wits and walked up to the small group. "Hi, Melody, I'm Dr. Stanford. This is Lizzie?"

Brock handed over the squalling infant. "She's been sick the past couple of days, but just a runny nose and a little fever. A couple of hours ago, she started screaming. I've tried everything," Melody explained.

The poor woman looked so frazzled and upset, Cassie gently patted her arm. "Let's go into my office and I'll examine her."

She led Melody into her office and set Lizzie down on the examination table. As she started checking the baby head to toe, she asked Melody questions to determine what could have prompted such a quick change of behavior.

Cassie checked the baby's ears, mouth and nose, listened to her heart and prodded her stomach for lumps. Nothing struck her as a possible cause for the screaming, and she was starting to worry that Melody and Lizzie might need to go to the emergency room. As Cassie checked the child's legs, though, her eyes landed on Lizzie's right pinkie toe, and she let out a quiet sigh of relief.

The toe was an angry reddish purple, and when Cassie looked closely, she found the culprit: a single strand of hair had become wound around the toe, cutting off the circulation and causing Lizzie's distress.

As soon as Cassie removed the hair, Lizzie quieted into sniffly sobs. Cassie held up the hair to the baby's mother, expecting her to be as relieved as Cassie was.

To Cassie's surprise, Melody burst into tears. Cassie

sat down beside her, Lizzie on her lap. The baby gurgled and reached out for her mama.

Melody grasped the baby and held her close, continuing to cry. "I never thought to look at her toes. I should have checked everywhere," Melody sobbed.

Cassie rubbed her shoulder lightly. "You did nothing wrong, Melody. You called a doctor as soon as you realized something was really off, which was the best thing you could do."

Melody's tears subsided at Cassie's words. "I'm sorry, Dr. Stanford," she said.

"Call me Cassie," Cassie said.

Melody smiled at her and wiped her eyes with a tissue Cassie offered her. "Cassie. I don't usually act like this. It's just... Lizzie's my everything. It broke my heart to see her cry like that."

Melody held her baby tight to her chest, where Lizzie gurgled happily, her good mood entirely restored.

"You're a caring mother," Cassie said.

Melody breathed out a long sigh. "It's difficult sometimes. I'm usually at work right now, but I stayed home today when she started screaming and panicked when it didn't get better. I thought maybe her cold was something worse, and I'd just ignored it."

Cassie could see that Lizzie's nose was running. "How about I check her now that she's calm so you can be sure it's just a cold?"

Melody's expression held such gratitude that Cassie took the baby without another word. After a careful examination of Lizzie, Cassie declared her healthy apart from a little cold. "Nothing to worry about," Cassie assured the young mother.

By the time Melody and Lizzie were gone, Cassie knew the boys must be home, though she'd been so absorbed with the appointment she hadn't heard anything outside of her office.

Cassie went in search of her children and Brock. It didn't take long to find them, though, as they were all sitting quietly on the living room floor, studying playing cards. Marshmallows were strewn about between them. What could they possibly be doing?

Before she could ask, Brock said, "I see your three and raise you three more," as he tossed six mini-marshmallows into the center of their little circle.

"You're playing poker? With marshmallows?" Cassie said in disbelief.

She couldn't decide if she was angry or not. She felt like she should be upset about her young boys gambling with little balls of sugar, but something about seeing the three of them together, clearly enjoying themselves, made it impossible.

Brock looked up at her from where he sat, his smile begging her not to be mad. "They wanted to learn how to play," he explained.

The boys looked up from their cards, faces still serious from concentration. Normally when she walked in after being away, they tackled her as soon as she entered. This time, though, they didn't budge from their spots, they were so intent on the game.

"They're *four*, you know," she reminded him, the corners of her lips sliding up involuntarily.

Brock shrugged. "Zach's got a great poker face," he said, as if that settled the matter.

"Me, too! I have a poker face!" Carter chirped.

Brock smiled at him, making Cassie's heart thump hard in her chest. "You've got Lady Luck on your side. I've never seen anyone get so many pairs," Brock told Carter, making the boy beam.

Cassie tried to reel in her emotions. "And the marshmallows?"

"We had to bet something," Brock said, as if it was the most obvious answer. "I figured using real money might make you mad."

"So marshmallows were clearly the best choice," she said, grinning so widely that her words couldn't possibly carry any bite to them.

"*Mini*-marshmallows. They're practically a vegetable. Plus, I'm planning to wipe them out before they get to eat any. I promise."

Cassie shook her head, but didn't say anything else. "You have ten more minutes to play and then we're having a *healthy* snack."

Cassie went into the kitchen and started slicing celery and carrots. She couldn't regret helping Melody, but she did wish she'd had a little more time alone with Brock. Just thinking about what could have happened sent shivers of excitement down her spine.

Well, they'd just have to wait. Though with only eight days left after this one, she was starting to wonder how they would ever manage to find another moment alone. Maybe having him hide under the bed wasn't such a bad idea—

Heavy footsteps behind her stopped her thoughts. Brock moved close, and when he leaned in to see what she was doing, his arm looped around her waist. "What are you making?" he asked, though she was sure he could very well see what it was.

She smiled and leaned into him for just a moment. Then another one. "Just your standard veggie plate," she told him. Finally she moved away. "Where are the boys?"

"Putting the cards away," he said, not stepping any closer, but not falling back, either.

She tried to think of something to talk about. Anything to keep her mind off how near he was. "The game ended pretty quickly. You cleaned out the four-year-olds already?" she asked.

His silence in response made her turn to look at him. His face was sheepish. "You didn't…lose, did you?" she asked, laughing.

"They kept going all-in, and when I called them, they'd hit the best hands. It was the most ridiculous luck I've ever seen."

Cassie just raised an eyebrow at him.

Brock grimaced. "I think your kids hustled me."

They both laughed, and were still laughing when Zach and Carter joined them, eager to tell their mother about their triumph.

As they all dug into the snack, the conversation turned to paint. "Can we paint our room now, Momma? Please!" Carter implored.

Cassie looked over at Brock. He said, "While you

were in with Melody, I got just about everything ready, so we can if you're up for it."

"It's decided," she told the twins. "Let's finish eating and then we'll paint your room the color of dragon scales."

BROCK OPENED THE paint cans while Cassie changed out of her scrubs. He wished she was still wearing her date dress, but even her grungiest paint-splattered jeans made her look so good, he wondered if she'd actually let him hide under the bed. The idea was sounding more and more reasonable.

To distract himself, Brock decided to mention the idea he'd gotten while playing poker with the boys. Once Cassie had them occupied outside of the room, as far from the paint as she could get them, he decided to talk to her about it.

"I don't know if you've ever considered getting a dog, but I think Zach and Carter would really love one," he commented as he began slathering one wall in the lurid green paint.

Cassie looked up at him from where she stood with her own roller, her eyebrows raised in surprise. "Did they say something to you about wanting a dog?"

"No," he said, "but dogs are great for kids on ranches. Though you don't need to if you think it'd be too much work."

"Actually, I think it's a great idea," she replied, turning back to her task.

"I bet my ma will watch the boys tomorrow for a few hours so we can go down to the shelter and pick one out without them knowing. I bet they'd love the surprise of coming home to find a dog waiting for them," he told her.

He could think of lots of amazing ways to spend a few hours alone with Cassie, but picking out a pet for her little boys seemed more important. For Cassie as well as Zach and Carter.

Cassie nodded, a small smile on her lips that he couldn't read. "What're you thinking?" he asked.

"It's just odd. You don't seem to dislike kids," Cassie said, not taking her eyes off the wall in front of her, "but I get the feeling you don't want any of your own."

Brock figured it was best to be as open as possible, just to be sure neither of them got any ideas about what could happen beyond the rodeo. "My life doesn't really work with children," he explained. "I like free-climbing cliffs and snowboarding down unmarked trails and skydiving, and I'd need to give all that up if I had a kid at home to worry about. I don't want any children of mine to go through what I did when my parents died."

Cassie nodded, but she didn't say anything. Clearly she had some thoughts on the subject.

"You can say it," Brock prompted her. "I've heard it all before from my ma."

Cassie shrugged. "I have no call to judge your lifestyle. I'm just a nine-day romance," she said, bumping him with her hip to show she was teasing.

"And I'm just your training wheels," he responded, bumping her back.

They glanced at each other, and Brock wasn't sure if they would start laughing or kissing. Neither happened, though, as Zach and Carter ran in at just that moment, looking around the room in amazement.

"You boys shouldn't be in here," Cassie warned.

"It's so cool!" Carter shouted.

"It smells bad," Zach said. "Is it always going to smell like that?"

Brock ruffled the boy's hair. "The smell will go away soon," Brock explained. "It's extra strong right now because the paint is still wet. Once we finish and let it dry, it won't be so strong."

"I don't want to sleep in here if it smells so bad," Zach said, looking upset.

"Once we're finished painting, I'll help you two get sleeping bags and you can sleep in the living room tonight. How does that sound?" Cassie asked Zach.

He still seemed concerned. "Can we sleep in your room?" he asked his mother.

Cassie paused for a moment before agreeing, and the boys raced off happily.

So much for hiding under the bed, Brock thought. Cassie must've been thinking the same thing, because she caught his eye, and when they grimaced at each other, they both burst into laughter.

Once the room was finished, Brock knew he needed to go home, as little as he wanted to. He consoled himself with the thought that he and Cassie would be alone the next day, even if they were spending that time picking out a dog. They'd manage a few kisses, and maybe…

Brock cleared his throat at the thought. Cassie looked

at him expectantly. "I should go," he told her. "With my siblings over and everything—".

"Of course," she said, though she sounded reluctant. "I don't have any patients tomorrow or anything, so as soon as you want to go on our errand, the boys will be ready."

Brock said goodbye to Zach and Carter and walked home. He looked back a couple of times, wishing he had an excuse to stay.

Before he walked in to his parents' house, Brock took stock of himself. He didn't want to give his siblings any hint as to what had happened that day. It was better if nobody knew, not even his family.

Which was why he felt so annoyed with Amy when he walked through the door and she immediately asked, "When's the wedding?"

Jose and Diego, who were sitting across from her on the couch, gave him twin smiles. "You didn't tell us you were getting married. Congratulations!" Jose said.

"I call best man," Diego added.

Jose looked scandalized and was clearly about to start an argument when Brock cut him off. "None of that. Don't any of you start rumors about me and Cassie."

He looked so fierce that Diego held up his hands. "We were just joking, Brock. We're your family—you know we won't do anything to hurt whatever it is you two have going on."

"Here's a pro-tip, though," Jose said. "If you want to keep a secret, maybe don't make out outside." He gestured out the window near where Amy sat with her foot propped on pillows.

"Inside your truck isn't super sneaky, either," Amy added.

Brock glanced out the window and saw immediately what they meant. From there, his siblings had a great view of Cassie's paddock and the driveway, too.

Brock shook his head, annoyed at himself. He should have thought of that, but it was too late now.

"Swear you won't say anything to anyone, not even Ma," Brock told them.

Amy rolled her eyes. "What are the chances Ma doesn't know already? I'm guessing around zero percent."

"Seriously, does being in love really make you that stupid?" Jose asked, which earned him a shove from his twin.

Jose fell off the couch with an "oomph!"

"I'm *not* in love, and you need to keep your mouth shut, Jose," Brock said aggressively, standing over his brother for a moment before stalking out of the room.

He found his ma and, to his relief, she said nothing about his and Cassie's apparently very public display of affection. All she did was agree to take care of the twins while Brock and Cassie went to the animal shelter. "I love those two boys. You let Cassie know that I'm happy to watch them anytime," she told Brock.

He wasn't sure if her comment was completely innocent or not, but he decided it was better not to ask.

Chapter Eleven

The next morning, when Brock and his ma prepared to go pick up the boys, Brock noticed that Amy was yet again sitting in front of the window, despite the early hour. There was a book in her lap, but her eyes were trained out the window, as if she was watching for someone or something. Had she been spying on him on purpose the day before, or was she standing vigil for another reason?

She didn't seem to be looking over at Cassie's house. Her eyes were on the street and their parents' driveway.

Now that he thought about it, that was where she would sit most of the time she was home, on the few occasions they had both been home at the same time in the past decade. "What're you watching for?" he asked her.

For a moment, Amy gave him a slightly panicked look, which just raised further questions, but she quickly controlled her expression and denied watching for anything. Their ma slapped Brock's arm. "You leave your sister alone and take me over to the Stanfords'. I've got some young children to spoil."

So Brock went with his mother, leaving Amy sitting beside the window. He considered trying to get his sister alone to figure out what she was doing, but the farther he got from the house, the more likely it seemed that he'd just imagined things. He dismissed the thoughts and focused on the task ahead of him.

"Thanks for taking the boys, Ma," Brock said as they tromped through the grass.

Sarah dismissed his gratitude with a wave of her hand. "Well, of course. Every young boy should have a dog. I'm proud of you for thinking of it."

"How do you know it wasn't Cassie's idea?" Brock asked.

His ma gave him a frown. "You don't think I know you well enough by now, boy?" she asked.

Brock laughed and put up his hands in surrender. "Sorry I questioned your clairvoyance."

She smacked him on the arm again and followed him onto Cassie's porch. Before he could knock, the door opened and Zach and Carter came tumbling out. "Nana Sarah" laughed in delight as she hugged them. "Do I ever have a fun day planned for you two," she said as she hustled them back toward her house.

"Be good!" Cassie called after them from inside the house.

"Should we get going?" Brock asked as he turned toward her.

He stopped, confused, when he noticed she was still wearing a bathrobe. Had she not expected him to be there so early?

Before he could ask, she grabbed his arm and pulled him into the house, closing the door behind him. At the same time, she tugged at the belt of the bathrobe, causing it to fall open and reveal black silk and lace beneath.

Brock's jaw dropped. "On the other hand," he said, wrapping his arms around her, "I think we have a few minutes."

WHEN THEY PARKED in front of the animal shelter a long while later, Cassie knew she was still grinning like an idiot, but she just couldn't get herself to stop. After what had happened that morning, she doubted she'd be able to stop smiling for a week.

Well, eight days to be exact. After that, Brock would be out of her life for good.

That thought was enough to bring down her mood a little. She reached for the truck door, but Brock was there opening it for her before she could, and he helped her down so gallantly that she blushed.

She needed to remind herself, for perhaps the tenth time that day, that this was all short-term. Not something she should get used to.

Cassie put her hands in her pockets to avoid the temptation to hold his, and together they walked into the animal shelter.

After speaking briefly with an employee, Cassie and Brock were ushered into a large area full of dozens of barking dogs in search of homes. Cassie wandered past the canines, trying to concentrate on finding the right one for Zach and Carter, not on the cowboy beside her who was cooing at the animals in a way that tugged at her heartstrings. If she let herself watch that, she might just fall for him, and *that* was certainly not allowed.

Temporary. Eight Days.

"How about this fella?" Brock asked her, bringing Cassie out of her thoughts.

He had stopped in front of a brown-and-white dog that was licking his fingers. After a few final kisses for Brock, the dog started running in circles, apparently proud of himself for completing his objective. She couldn't help but laugh.

"This is Freckles," the worker explained. "He's mostly beagle. A very happy dog, and he probably won't get much bigger. Good for young children."

Cassie agreed. The boys would love Freckles. The worker opened the cage and Freckles jumped into her arms, his tongue all over her face and every part he could get at. She hugged him close, then turned to Brock.

"He looks like a winner to me," Brock said, rubbing the furry little head.

Freckles wiggled in Cassie's arms, trying to get close enough to Brock to give him another thorough licking.

After signing enough documents to make her question if she was adopting a dog or a child, Cassie paid for a final vet check and vaccinations and was told she'd be able to pick up Freckles the next day.

Finally, Cassie and Brock left the animal shelter. Cassie wondered what time it was, and if she should go pick up Zach and Carter right away. She wasn't sure if she wanted more time with Brock alone or to have her young chaperones back as soon as possible.

If she was being honest, she was a little nervous. Now that things between them had finally gotten physical—*really* physical—she knew it would be hard to give it all up in only one short week. It almost seemed easier and smarter to stop it now, before she completely fell for him.

Cassie knew she wouldn't stop their relationship, though, regardless of how smart it might be. She'd enjoy every second of it, whatever it did to her once he'd left.

As soon as they buckled in, Brock asked, "So, how are you going to get free long enough to pick up Freckles tomorrow?"

"I spoke with Jack Stuart this morning, actually, and planned on Zach and Carter going over to his ranch for a half-day horse camp. Your brothers are going to have their equipment over to cut and bale the hay," she explained.

She didn't say that she'd only decided to send the boys to camp *after* her date with Brock in order to give them another opportunity to be alone. Judging by the sly look on his face, he seemed to guess as much.

"Jose and Diego will want us to stay out of the way while that's going on," he said, not explaining where they could be or what they could do while the machinery operated in the yard.

He didn't need to.

"So, are we heading straight to my house to pick up Zach and Carter?" Brock asked.

Cassie wanted to say no, but their morning trip had lasted well into the afternoon, in no small part to her black negligee. "Yeah," she said, trying not to sound deflated.

It was silly, of course, to want Brock again so soon.

It had just been a few hours since they'd been together in her bed, creating memories she was sure would last her many lonely nights.

Still, she couldn't help but desire him even more, now that she knew what she'd been missing. It wasn't just that he was good in bed—though that certainly seemed to be the case—it was the two of them together that made it spectacular. Just as they worked well together when painting a room or making repairs, they worked well together in all physical aspects, apparently.

If only their lives harmonized, too, she thought with a silent sigh. Unfortunately, their lives were halves of two very different jigsaw puzzles, and trying to shove them together would be an impossible task.

How had she gotten on that topic again? Cassie had found herself going over the same well-worn tracks of thinking again and again, and it was getting wearisome; they had a week left together, end of story.

"Don't tell Pop you're taking Zach and Carter to the Stuarts' for horse camp," Brock said, breaking into her thoughts.

Cassie was confused for a second before realizing what he meant. Brock's adopted father ran his own horse camp. "Whoops. I completely forgot. Is that a problem?"

"No, probably not, but it's best not to bring it up. We've been telling him for a while now that he should hire more help, that the camp is too much for him. He's a little sensitive about it. Thinks we're calling him old."

Cassie agreed not to say anything, then looked out the window to see her home as they passed. For one wild moment, she considered telling Brock to stop and turn in. Another half hour together before they picked up the boys couldn't hurt, could it?

They continued on and parked in front of his parents' without her saying anything, though. As they climbed out of Brock's truck, Cassie felt a twinge of regret. Not only for deciding to collect the boys immediately, but also because Brock's truck would no longer be parked in front of her house. It was silly, she knew, but she liked having it there. It was a reminder that he would be coming back.

Before she could dive down that hole any further, her sons ran out the door. She braced herself for a high-speed hug, but the boys veered from her and went straight to Brock.

"DID YOU REALLY ride a bull when you were twelve years old?" Carter asked.

Brock looked up at his ma, Jose and Diego, who were all standing in the doorway. "What have you been telling them?" he asked.

"Only the truth," Diego answered. "They asked what you were like when you were a kid, so we told them."

Brock wondered if anything had been mentioned about his parents' death—he could easily imagine Jose saying something without really thinking about it—but there was no way to ask at the moment. Not with Zach and Carter right there.

"We should go," Cassie said, breaking into the moment.

Brock automatically turned to go with her before he

realized he should probably stay home. His whole family rarely got together, and everyone would be leaving in a couple days. Plus, it might seem suspicious to everyone if he left, and he didn't need any more of that going on. "I'll come by tomorrow morning for…"

Brock trailed off, not able to say where the boys were going nor bring up the errand he'd run with Cassie. Cassie nodded. "We'll be leaving a little before nine. Just come in whenever. The door will be unlocked."

Brock wondered if she was giving him a coded message, telling him to sneak over that night after Zach and Carter were asleep.

No, she couldn't mean that, could she? She *had* surprised him that morning with that sexy black outfit.

Then again, Cassie had made it plenty clear that her kids came first, and that might include keeping their distance from each other when the boys were nearby, even if they were asleep.

Brock didn't know, which meant he wouldn't be going over there tonight, much as he might want to. It was best to err on the side of caution, to avoid stepping on her toes and ruining the whole thing. Even if it wouldn't last beyond a few more days, he didn't want to do anything to spoil it for either of them.

Finally, when Cassie and her boys had disappeared into their house, Brock turned back to his family. They all acted as if they hadn't been watching him, but they were doing a bad job of it. A little reluctantly, he followed them into the house.

Chapter Twelve

Cassie tucked Zach and Carter into bed that night with excitement pooling in her belly, even though she knew the chances that Brock would come over were slim. She couldn't be sure that he'd understood what she meant when she said the door would be unlocked, or that even if he did, he'd be able or willing to sneak out of his parents' house.

All of it made her feel like a teenager trying to arrange an illicit tryst, and she loved it. The entire afternoon, even when she was on the phone making appointments for two more new patients, she could hardly focus on anything but to wish for night to come faster.

Cassie had never been one for this sort of behavior as a teen, and she didn't even start dating until she was in college. Even then it was all fairly rational and well-behaved. This time, she didn't want to be well-behaved. If she was going to have this once-in-a-lifetime kind of connection for a limited time, by God, she wanted to get as much out of it as she could.

Cassie turned out Zach and Carter's light and closed the door. She went and checked once more that the front door was unlocked, though she'd already made sure at least five times, and then she went to her room.

After sifting through her pajama options carefully, Cassie settled on a long-ish shirt—no pants—and climbed into bed with a book. She tried to read, but it was nearly impossible. What if she ended up sitting there pretending to read and he never showed up?

What if he did?

Cassie was almost starting to regret this situation for herself when she heard a very quiet *click*. Her heart stopped in anticipation.

Maybe it was one of the boys getting up to go to the bathroom.

Still, she set down her book and waited eagerly.

Brock appeared in the doorway, cowboy hat on his head and boots in his hand, looking a little unsure. "If you don't want me to be here—"

Before he could finish the sentence, she had jumped out of bed and closed the distance between them. In short order, the door was closed and the light was off, and the butterflies in Cassie's stomach changed to molten ecstasy.

When Cassie awoke, it was still dark, but she could hear small noises coming from a few feet away. She picked up her phone and looked at it blearily. It was just past four in the morning. Brock knelt beside her and brushed her hair out of her face. "Hey," he whispered softly.

She pressed her cheek against his hand like a cat and smiled, even though he wouldn't be able to see it in the dark. "I didn't want to wake you, but I should get back before anybody gets up. You still have a couple more hours before you need to be up, though."

She wanted him to stay. What if he just stayed? For the next day and the night after that and the night after that—

No, that wouldn't work, of course.

So Cassie just nodded, enjoyed one last kiss that she could feel all the way to her toes and then said goodbye.

After he was gone, her bed felt unpleasantly empty, and Cassie wondered if this romance was such a good idea after all. Just as with every time that thought had come up before, she knew she would take every second with Brock McNeal she could get.

Even if it was only for another seven days.

BROCK WALKED INTO Cassie's house the next morning after checking to see that the door was still unlocked. Though it felt a little odd, it was nice, too, and the memories of the night before flooded through him pleasantly. He pushed them away, though, because today would be about Zach and Carter, not him and Cassie.

The living room was empty, so he went to the kitchen in search of the home's occupants. Nobody was there, either, but it also felt cool and inviting, and he lingered there for a moment, enjoying the atmosphere of a quiet country home. His tiny apartment in Dallas lacked any feeling of home—though a good deal of that probably had to do with how little he was there. Being out on the rodeo circuit for months at a time kept him from ever feeling really settled. Heck, he'd probably slept in his truck more times than he'd slept in his own bed.

But there was more to it than that. This wasn't just a kitchen in anybody's house. This was Cassie's kitchen, which already showed signs of her personality despite the boxes still sitting in the corner. A blue spoon rest with painted daisies all over it sat beside the stove, and an oven mitt that looked like a dinosaur's mouth, complete with cloth teeth, hung on the wall. He could imagine her attacking Carter with it before pulling something out of the oven.

He felt a sudden twinge of wistfulness and walked out of the kitchen toward the hallway. He needed to find Cassie, so he started walking toward her bedroom. Just the thought of being alone in there with her again sent adrenaline through his veins, but he knew the boys were somewhere close by, and that fantasy was going to need to wait.

As he walked down the hall, he stopped when he heard murmuring through the open doorway of the twins' room. Glancing inside, he saw Cassie, Zach and Carter on the floor, driving toy cars around on a rug covered in street designs, each one occasionally screeching to a halt or flipping over in dramatic car crashes. Cassie looked beautiful, the lack of sleep from the night before undetectable. It even seemed like her smile was brighter than usual, and there was a glitter in her eye that he liked to think was his doing.

Or maybe she was just enjoying playing with her sons, he thought when he saw her car fly into the air as she laughed. That sound rolled through him as only her laugh could. He watched the little family, not wanting to spoil the moment.

Then Carter saw him and ran over with a car in his

hand. "Here," he told Brock, handing him the tiny car. "You can use the red one."

"Momma said we could play cars until it was time to go because we got ready early," Zach said.

Brock understood he was expected to play cars with them, though it was a strange thing, to drive tiny cars along tiny streets. Still, he dutifully knelt down on the floor and started running the car along one of the streets, feeling a little foolish.

"This isn't really your thing, is it?" Cassie asked him under her breath.

No good answer came to him, so he simply replied, "I usually drive a truck, myself."

"Here's a truck!" Zach said, dropping a small silver truck in front of Brock.

Brock picked up the truck and studied it. "This is actually pretty similar to mine," he commented.

"Yeah," Zach said. "I got it with Aunt Emma. She said we could have one car each, but I picked a truck instead because it looks like yours."

Brock stared at the young boy for a few seconds, astonished. These two kids constantly surprised him.

"There you go," Cassie said, her voice soft. "Now you have a truck to drive that's just like yours."

Brock could only nod, and for several seconds, the only sounds were the explosions the boys created as they slammed vehicles together.

"Where is your truck going?" Carter asked Brock as he drove along the street. "To the rodeo to ride bulls?"

He sounded so excited about the prospect of bull riding that Brock's mind whirred quickly. There was no way he was going to encourage Carter's newfound obsession with riding bulls. "Nope," he told Carter. "My truck is going to the carnival to ride the Ferris wheel and eat cotton candy. Maybe while he's there he'll play one of the games and try to win your momma a stuffed animal."

Carter's car pulled up alongside Brock's. "Me, too! I want to go to the carnival, too!"

"We like carnivals, don't we?" Cassie asked her sons, who both nodded.

"Well, you missed the spring fair, which is big and not too far away. But the Halloween carnival will be here before you know it."

"Will you take us?" Zach asked, looking straight at Brock.

"I…" he started, but he didn't know what to say.

He was leaving town soon, but he could come back for the Halloween carnival. Brock could just imagine Zach and Carter picking out pumpkins and screaming at the top of their lungs as they all whirled around on the teacups.

Or would it just be better to make a clean break and avoid all three of them as much as possible? His heart and his brain had two very different answers.

And none of that addressed the fact that Cassie might not even want him around after these few days were over. Once she was done with her training wheels, she might be ready for something more permanent with somebody else.

Cassie looked Zach in the eye, her face serious. "Remember what we talked about? How Brock needs to go back to work and won't be around anymore?"

Zach looked glum, but he nodded. Brock couldn't feel worse if he tried.

CASSIE LOOKED AT the man and two boys. They were all still moving their vehicles around, but none of them seemed very happy at the prospect of Brock moving on.

He didn't contradict her, though, so it was clear that was still the plan. Seven more days together, and then he'd be off for the rodeo.

"We should get going," Cassie said as she stood, pushing away her unpleasant thoughts. "It's time for horse camp!"

Zach and Carter jumped up, their good moods restored at the thought of horses. "Will we get to ride one?" Carter asked eagerly.

"I don't know. What do you think, Brock?" she asked, trying to turn his mood around, too.

Brock seemed to think carefully about the question, the way people often did around very young children. It was clear he was catching on quick. "I'm not sure how the Stuarts run their camp, but I'm guessing you'll meet the horses first, pet them, learn about them, and after all that you *might* ride them. But only if you feel ready for it."

Cassie could tell his last sentence was directed toward Zach, who seemed a little nervous at the prospect of hopping onto a horse's back. For all his agreement with Carter's talk about bull riding, Zach would need a bit of time before he was ready to ride any large animal.

Soon they were all settled into Cassie's SUV and on their way to the Stuart Ranch. While the boys discussed camp noisily in the back, Brock sat quietly in the passenger seat. Cassie redirected her thoughts away from the cowboy beside her and onto the tasks for the day. Buy bedding, toys and food for Freckles; then get him from the shelter. By the time he was settled at home, it would likely be time to pick up the boys.

She tried not to feel too disappointed about that. She'd had more amazing times in Brock's arms than most people got in their entire lives, so could she really complain if they had no opportunity to be alone that day?

Cassie knew the answer to that. Of course she could complain, as long as she was the only one to hear it.

When she pulled onto the dirt driveway of the Stuart Ranch, Zach and Carter climbed out. They shouted their goodbyes and thundered toward the small group of young children surrounding Grandma Stuart. Cassie waved to their retreating backs and put her car in reverse.

"I wish we had time to say hi to Rosalind and Diamond," Cassie said, "but we have too much to do to get the dog settled before camp is over."

Cassie hoped Brock wouldn't say anything about the boys being sad he was leaving. Frankly, she was, too, and she didn't want to talk about it. Better to enjoy the little time they had.

"I think they're going to be over the moon about Freckles," Brock said.

Cassie was relieved, and they talked about the silly

dog the entire way to the pet shop. As they walked through the giant store, Cassie and Brock laughed and argued good-naturedly as they chose the perfect bedding, food and collar for little Freckles. "This pup is going to be pretty spoiled for a ranch dog, I imagine," Brock commented as they dropped a half-dozen toys into their already full cart.

Cassie knew she should watch her spending more carefully, but now that the hay was being baled and she had a few patients, she couldn't help but feel more secure, and she was willing to splurge on the adorable mutt. "I think he'll prefer relaxing in his bed and terrorizing the house over herding cattle. Maybe I'll need to get another dog someday just for that purpose."

Brock smiled at her. "You're going to have cattle?"

"A pretty smart cowboy mentioned it to me once, and I think it's a good idea," she said, thinking back to the day they'd walked along the fences.

It had been only a few days before, but so much had happened since then.

"I think we can get your paddock finished in a day or two if we really put in the time, and then Diamond and Rosalind can come home," Brock told her, clearly thinking about that walk, too.

With the rush to finish her office, that had been pushed to the wayside. If they could get it done, though, her ranch would be on its way to matching her dream.

And they only had seven days before he left, so time was not her friend.

Brock picked up a container of dog biscuits and tossed it in the heaping cart on their way to the cashier.

"How about we buckle down on that tomorrow? Amy's leaving in the morning, but after that, I've got the entire day free. We should be able to fix it and paint it, if we're quick about it, and maybe even pick up the horses the day after," he said.

Cassie agreed, then turned to her current objective: becoming a dog owner.

And that seemed to be a much more expensive task than she'd previously thought, judging by the numbers jumping up on the cash register. She was starting to re-think the dozen top-of-the-line dog bones and the collar with the studs when Brock whipped out his credit card.

"Got a splinter there, Brock?" she asked, blocking the credit card machine with her hand.

Brock rolled his eyes at her attempt to keep him from paying. "It was my idea for you to get a dog. You'll have to clean up his poop every day. I should at least pay for his bedding, even if you decided against the one with the horseshoe pattern."

After a brief argument, she relented, secretly happy she didn't need to put anything back in order to pay for it. Soon, the items were packed into the back of her car and they were off to get Freckles.

When they parked in front of the shelter, Cassie turned to Brock. "Ready to pick up a dog?" she asked.

Then she noticed that he was distracted, looking out the window back the way they'd just driven. Before she could ask him what he'd seen, he turned back to her and gave her a kiss that made her toes curl. "You grab Freckles. I'll meet you back here faster than green grass through a goose."

He got out of the car and was gone before she could recover her wits and understand what he'd said enough to find out where he was going.

All Cassie could do was wonder at his behavior, as well as his choice in idioms, and smile because of the kiss as she greeted Freckles, who seemed even more excited and loving than the day before, if that was possible.

By the time Freckles was secured in his crate in the back seat of the car, Brock was back, a large box in his arms. "Don't ask," he said the moment she opened her mouth.

Cassie closed her mouth again and got in the car. Brock seemed very happy with himself, so she could only imagine he'd purchased something ridiculous for the dog and wanted it to be a surprise. Probably something cowboy-themed to make up for her vetoing his choice of dog bed.

They got back to her place and unloaded all the purchases, except for one. Brock left the mystery box in the car, warning her not to touch it.

As Cassie had feared, by the time Freckles was settled in, it was time to pick up the boys. She started to say goodbye to the dog when Brock shook his head. "How about I go get the boys? That way you can be here waiting for them with Freckles."

Cassie loved the idea, so she tossed Brock her keys and settled in to wait, petting the sweet little animal, whom she already considered part of the family. Freckles scrambled into her lap and snuggled close, licking her hand at every opportunity.

Almost as soon as Brock left, Cassie's phone rang. A quick glance told her it was Emma.

"Hello?" she said.

"Hey Cassie, Daniel Forrester needs to come in for a doctor's appointment."

Cassie could hear bickering in the background and Emma say, "Yes, you do, so stop being a baby, Danny."

The name sounded familiar. "Danny's your cousin, right?"

Emma had told Cassie about her cousin who was currently staying in the tiny apartment above her bakery until he "got settled in town," in Emma's words.

"Yep, my cousin. He has some weird pain in his leg every once in a while, and despite what he says, he should get it checked out," Emma explained, though it sounded like she was talking more to her cousin than to Cassie.

"Is it something he should go to the hospital about?" Cassie asked.

"Listen," Emma said quietly, "I'll be lucky if I can get him to go see you. There's no way he's going to the hospital unless you tell him it's life-or-death. Which it could be!" she exclaimed much louder, likely in the direction of Danny.

Cassie tried not to laugh. "Do you want to bring him in right away, or can it wait until after Mrs. Edelman's appointment next week?"

"Next week would be great. He will see you then." Emma said.

Cassie laughed as she heard Emma say, "Yes, you will!" to her cousin as she shut off the phone.

That was going to be an interesting appointment.

Good. Anything to keep her mind off Brock leaving.

She had already scheduled three other appointments for the same day as Mrs. Edelman's. The day after the rodeo.

It just seemed best to keep herself busy.

Luckily, she heard the car pull up and was able to get her mind onto Freckles and her children. Better topics, for sure.

The door opened and Freckles jumped out of her lap, running toward the noise as Zach and Carter ran into the house. They entered the living room with Brock behind them, amazed at the dog that came up to greet them.

"A puppy!" Zach shouted as he and Carter kneeled down to meet Freckles.

Cassie was just as surprised as they were. "Where did you get those hats?" she asked.

The boys were both sporting child-size cowboy hats. They were so enthralled in the dog that they didn't hear her question, but the answer became obvious when she saw that Brock was holding another hat. He held it out to her. "I thought they should have cowboy hats after their first real horse experience. And you should have one, too, now that you're a rancher."

She no longer had any doubt about what his mysterious box contained. She didn't know what to say as he placed the hat on her head, and it took everything in her not to pull him into a kiss right then and there.

"Thank you," she said, her voice soft as she held back happy tears.

He just smiled back and tipped his own hat, the grown-up version of Zach and Carter's, at her. Then he turned to watch the boys play with their new dog. Cassie did after a moment, too.

"Is he ours forever?" Zach asked, looking at her with wide eyes, his hands low so Freckles could lick them.

Cassie nodded. "Yep, he's our dog now. We adopted him. His name's Freckles."

"Freckles is a silly name," Carter commented.

Cassie worried there was going to be a whole argument over the pup's name, but Brock kneeled down next to them and said, "There's a rodeo bull with the same name. Crazy fella. I've been lucky enough that I haven't ever tried to ride him. He'd chew me up and spit me out."

Zach and Carter's eyes grew wide, "Really?" Zach asked.

"A bull named Freckles?" Carter added.

He nodded. "Yep. Freckles."

"Cool!" they said in unison, then bent back down to the dog.

Brock stood again and smiled at Cassie. Once he was close enough that they wouldn't be overheard, she whispered, "There isn't really a scary bull named Freckles, right?"

Brock put a hand over his heart. "God's honest truth."

Cassie laughed.

The rest of the evening was spent gathered around the new puppy, exclaiming at every wag of his tail, and the boys chattering excitedly about horse camp. Finally, though, she saw that the boys' eyes were drooping and she looked at the clock. "It's past your bedtime, guys. Go brush your teeth and I'll put Freckles away in his crate."

Zach and Carter protested, but once they saw that their mother wasn't going to budge, they got up and did as she said. On their way out of the room, Carter walked up to Brock and craned his head so he could look the grown man in the eyes. "Will you tell us a bedtime story about riding in the rodeo?" Carter asked.

Cassie was about to cut in, reassuring Brock he didn't need to and placating Carter with a bedtime story about their father, but before she could say anything, Brock was ruffling Carter's hair. "Sure, buddy," he said.

Carter and Zach ran off to brush their teeth, looking excited.

Cassie said nothing as she settled Freckles down for the night, but her heart felt twisted tight inside her. She was touched by her boys' attachment to Brock, but at the same time saddened that in just a few days they would need to say goodbye.

IN ONLY A few short minutes, the two boys lay in their bunks, looking expectantly at Brock. For a moment he felt a kind of stage fright. They were just so attentive. At least he had some good stories.

"One time a few years back," he began, "I was all set to ride a bull named Whirlwind. He was the biggest, meanest bull I'd ever had to ride."

"Were you scared?" Zach asked in a whisper, his eyes the size of saucers.

Brock wanted to laugh at how serious the boy was, but he held it in. "Sure I was scared. Wouldn't you be?"

Zach nodded solemnly.

"But I'd prepared and practiced, and I wasn't about to give up just because I was scared."

"Did you get hurt?" Carter asked, leaning forward in his bed.

"No, but it was a close thing. I thought I was going to get thrown the moment they opened the chute, but I managed to stay on for the whole eight seconds."

"Did you win?" Cassie asked.

Brock looked over to see her leaning against the green wall of the room, listening to the story. He smiled at her. "Yep. Biggest purse I ever got."

"I want to ride bulls!" Carter exclaimed.

"Me, too!" Zach said.

As much as Brock enjoyed riding on the circuit, the idea of these sweet little boys jumping on the back of a crazy bull was too much for him. "Whoa, pardners," he said. "My story isn't over yet."

The two settled down as Brock tried to come up with something to add that might keep them from bull riding. His most recent ride came back to him, and he told the boys, "After I jumped off the bull and was waving to the crowd, Whirlwind got free and came after me!"

"Oh, no!" Zach shouted.

"Oh, yes," Brock said as seriously as he could. "He stomped his big scary hoof this close to my head." He held up his finger and thumb an inch apart. "And I learned that riding bulls can be very very dangerous and should only be done by people who practice a lot."

Zach and Carter seemed satisfied with the ending and snuggled down in their beds. Cassie went over and kissed each of them good-night, and then she walked with Brock down the hallway, toward the door. "Whirlwind didn't *really* almost kill you, right?" she asked.

"Nah. I just added that at the end," he said, feeling a twinge of guilt at the omission that it had happened with another bull just a few days ago.

Cassie seemed relieved. At the door, Cassie put her hand against his chest and they shared a long, lingering kiss. Brock almost asked to stay, but he knew she would say yes and he wasn't sure if he could make himself leave in the middle of the night again. Plus, his sister had her flight out of the country early in the morning. He needed to be home.

Still, he didn't want to go. If he went home, the next time he saw her, they'd only have six more days left.

But he said good-night and turned away, pausing for a long moment to wait for the click of the lock that never came, and then he walked slowly back to his parents' house, his mind whirling between Cassie, her unlocked door and his interactions with the twins.

He'd always said he didn't want children, but Zach and Carter made something tug inside him he hadn't felt before. Was he willing to make children a part of his life, even if it meant leaving them without a father?

He pictured a bull's hoof slamming down next to his head, a slip of his hand while rock climbing that nearly dropped him a thousand feet, his motorcycle sliding around cars at breakneck speeds.

No. He couldn't do that to kids. He *knew* that, so why was this suddenly a question for him?

Brock reached the dark house and closed the door behind him, wishing he could shut out the feelings that had followed him home. He took off his cowboy hat, leaned against the door and drew in a deep breath, letting it out slowly.

"What's going on, Brock?" Amy asked.

Brock looked around, surprised. He'd thought he was alone and hadn't noticed his sister sitting in the corner of the room, working on her laptop, her foot propped high as usual. She closed her computer. "You aren't really falling in love with her, are you?" she asked, her voice worried.

He wanted to answer that he wasn't, but he knew it would sound like a lie. "Maybe," he said. "But it doesn't matter. Neither of us is looking for anything long-term."

He didn't want to really examine his feelings for Cassie. "She has kids, which is the main problem," he said.

"Oh, yeah, your no-kids rule," Amy responded.

"I just don't want to leave some kids without a father, okay?" he said.

He knew he was sounding defensive, but it was true.

He thought it best to change the topic. "Do you do dangerous stuff while you're out there in the world?" he asked, thinking back to a conversation he'd had with their ma a few days before.

Amy looked at him thoughtfully. "I don't hide in my hotel room, if that's what you mean. But dangerous? Not particularly. I like to travel, but that doesn't mean

I have a death wish or anything. I write about interesting places, not about free-climbing cliffs or jumping out of airplanes."

Brock tried to hide his grimace. He'd done both of those things in the last couple of years. Did that mean he had a death wish?

It wasn't a question he wanted to know the answer to.

"Listen, Brock, do you *want* to have kids?" Amy asked.

Brock's answer a few days before was a firm no. Now, though…

"Do you?" he asked, more to delay answering than anything else.

"We're not talking about me here," she said.

Brock knew Amy well enough to know when she was holding something back, and this was definitely one of those times. He was about to ask her what it was when she stood up, careful to keep her weight off her sore ankle. "I'm going to bed," she said, grabbing a crutch that their pop had found somewhere in the attic.

Brock guessed she'd known what he was going to ask and considered stopping her, but he just said goodnight and let her leave the room. If she didn't want to tell him, that was her choice.

Brock glanced out the window and saw that Cassie's bedroom light was still on, and he put his hat back on. Whatever self-control he had left him, and he knew he'd need to find some way to leave Cassie's arms before morning.

What else could he do?

Chapter Thirteen

Brock felt bleary-eyed and sleepy when he woke up in his bed the next day, which wasn't surprising since he'd now gone two nights with only a few hours' sleep. But he needed to get up to say goodbye to Amy, and then he had a paddock to fix.

He wasn't sure whether or not to ask Amy about their conversation the night before, but ultimately he decided not to say anything. His sister had always played her cards close to the chest, and he'd learned long ago not to push her to talk about something she wasn't ready to share.

Brock knocked lightly on her bedroom door. She opened it, and he could see her backpack and suitcase ready to go behind her. "Want some help?" he asked.

Normally, she'd punch him on the arm and explain how she managed to haul her belongings across the globe, and she could probably make it down the stairs, too. But hobbling as she was, she just nodded and he grabbed her things.

Brock went first down the stairs, carrying Amy's bags, ready to help if she had trouble, but between the crutch and the handrail she was able to maneuver them just fine. Pop was waiting at the bottom of the steps and took her things out to the truck. Amy and Brock went to the dining room, where Ma had laid out quite a feast for breakfast, including waffles and syrup. He wasn't sure if Ma did that as a treat for his sister, or if it was more of a last-ditch effort to bribe her to stay longer with the promise of sweets.

Soon, the whole family was gathered around the table. With the twins about to leave for Dallas to work on their business and Amy heading to Morocco, Brock's parents seemed quieter than usual. He felt for them and vowed to spend more time at home from now on. He could probably come visit every couple of weeks, if he put in the effort.

He tried to believe this thought had nothing to do with Cassie, but it wasn't easy to convince himself that he didn't want more time with her.

Six days just didn't seem long enough.

Brock turned his thoughts back to his family. "When are you coming back, Ames?" he asked.

She swallowed, but didn't look up from her plate. "Actually, I'll be back in the fall, I think."

There was a clatter as their ma dropped her fork. "So soon? For how long?"

Brock could see that Ma was trying not to get her hopes up. Amy still kept her eyes on her plate, not looking at their mother. She looked pale. "I'm not sure. It's still up in the air."

Everyone around the table waited for her to say more, for Ma to prod her, but both women remained quiet. Finally, Pop said, "We love having you here, you know that. Stay as long as you can."

With that, the conversation was finished. Brock wondered what could be bringing his sister back to Spring Valley after so short a time, when for the past decade she'd made a habit of visiting once a year or less.

But, as usual, Amy didn't say anything else and Brock didn't ask. There was no point pressing her about it and the entire family knew it.

After breakfast, Amy said goodbye to Jose, Diego and Ma. Brock walked out with her as Pop started up the truck. Brock could hear Ma sniffing behind him, and she knew the woman was unsuccessfully holding back tears. From the expression on Amy's face, she knew it, too.

Brock was glad his brothers were staying the rest of the day, or he knew Ma would be nearly inconsolable.

At the truck, Brock kissed Amy on the cheek. "I'll miss you," he told her. "If you're back in the fall, I'll try to be here. We can spend a little more time just you and me, what do you say?"

Brock knew that if given the chance, he would spend time with Cassie then, too, but he didn't say it aloud.

"It's been a long time since we hung out, hasn't it?" Amy said, wiping away a quick tear.

Brock hadn't really thought about it, but it was true. In middle and high school, they had been good friends. Even when he left for the circuit as she finished her senior year, they had stayed in touch.

It must've been the summer after she graduated,

when she left for college, that things had changed. How had he not noticed that?

Brock wished he had realized it sooner, that he and Amy could talk before she needed to leave, but she was already climbing gingerly into Pop's truck. Next time, he vowed.

"Bye, sis," he said.

Amy opened her window and gave him one last searching gaze. "Be careful with Cassie," she told him, her eyes serious and a little sad.

Did she think Cassie was dangerous somehow? He didn't know what to say to that. Amy seemed to realize he was confused, because she added, "With your heart, I mean. Love isn't always what it's cracked up to be."

Then she rolled the window up and turned to their pop, and the truck started moving. Brock watched, trying to absorb what she'd said. What had happened to Amy to make her say something like that? It was too late to ask, though. All he could do was wave.

She waved back, and then they were gone.

Brock walked back inside to find his ma sitting at the table with Diego. He had no idea where Jose was, but Brock guessed he was out at the barn or something. He never did well with emotions. That was Diego's job.

"Hey, Ma," Brock said, sitting on the other side of her.

The woman looked up at him and brushed away a tear. "What are you still doing here, Brock? Didn't you say you and Cassie would be fixing the paddock today so she could get her horses home for good and all?"

"Well, yes, but—" he started.

Surely she didn't expect him to leave her there in tears?

Apparently, she did. "You get along, then. That woman needs your help much more than I do. Go on, get!"

Brock stood, simultaneously concerned for his ma and happy to be going to see Cassie. Even though it had only been a few hours since he'd held her, it felt like much too long.

Along the short walk between the two houses, Brock's mind wandered back to his sister and the rest of his family.

The concept of family had never been something super important to Brock—he loved his siblings and the parents who raised him, but it had never mattered much if he saw them twice a month or twice a year. Now, suddenly, he felt an ache for that kind of closeness he never quite got on the circuit, even with his uncle Joe coaching him.

Or maybe he was feeling the desire for a family of his own.

If so, it was just a temporary feeling, brought on by the amount of time he was spending with Cassie and her children. Nothing could come of it in the end, he knew. Even if he could convince Cassie to see him occasionally when he was in town, eventually she would find someone who could be the husband and father she and the boys deserved.

She was too kind and loving, and the boys were too wonderful in their own right for her to stay single for very long.

Brock didn't like that thought one bit, and he was relieved to feel his phone buzz as a welcome distraction. It was Jay, texting him about the mines.

I've got five guys who want to go with us and all the rope we might need. Do you have your climbing gear with you? It could come in handy.

Brock's climbing gear was piled in a duffel with his rodeo stuff, gathering dust since he got to Spring Valley. Just like everything else not connected to working on Cassie's ranch.

Brock sent a quick affirmative, then put his phone away. He was walking up the porch by that point and didn't want Cassie or the boys to see. He was worried Cassie would find out what he had planned and be disapproving, but he was even more concerned the twins would think it was cool and exciting and try something like that themselves.

He'd never forgive himself if they got hurt doing something foolish like that.

Inside the house, he quickly found the little family on the floor doting over their new pet. He was glad to see them all wearing their new cowboy hats. He'd bought them on a whim, and it gave him a good feeling to know all three of them liked the gift.

Something to remember him by. He quickly dismissed that depressing thought. He'd see them again. Even if it wasn't the same, even if Cassie *did* find someone who would be a good husband and father, they would still be his parents' neighbors.

The knowledge didn't help much.

Cassie looked up and saw him, and the way her expression brightened as their eyes connected made his heart thump.

He was going to make these six days count. Solid fencing, a repaired barn, mended house and as many nights in each other's arms as he could get.

"Are we working on the paddock today?" Cassie asked, standing.

"You bet," Brock replied, and soon the four people and one rambunctious puppy were outside in the morning heat.

While the boys tried unsuccessfully to teach Freckles to fetch, Brock and Cassie began working on the fencing around the paddock, checking each piece of wood, using the crowbar to pull off any that needed to be replaced and nailing up new ones. Cassie never once complained about the hard work, and it went quickly.

Just like in every other situation, Brock and Cassie worked seamlessly together. In just under three hours, they had managed to do what Brock had thought would take an entire day or more.

By the time they were finished, everyone was starving and Brock was happier than ever about purchasing hats for everyone, since the sun had been beating down on them relentlessly the entire time.

After food and time to cool off, they once more braved the heat to paint the paddock so it would be completely ready for Rosalind and Diamond, who they'd decided should come home the next day.

Zach and Carter were reluctant to go back out in the

heat, so Brock sent a quick text to his ma, who scurried over to take Freckles and the twins to her house for ice cream—and general spoiling—while their mother and Brock labored in the sun.

By the time they were done, neither of them wanted anything more than a cool shower. And, since the boys were still secure in Nana Sarah's clutches, that was just what they did.

That night, when Brock returned after the twins were asleep, he found Cassie dozing on her bed, the light still on. He was about to leave when she woke up enough to hold her arms out to him, so he turned out the light, slid into bed with her and slept hard until just before dawn.

And then there were only five days left.

The next day rushed by in a flurry of activity as Rosalind and Diamond got settled in. Brock helped Cassie prepare stalls for them in the barn, and they repaired anything in the barn they could get their hands on, all while Brock instructed Cassie on everything he knew about horse care and maintenance.

Another sunset, another late-night entrance, another few hours in Cassie's arms.

Four days left.

CASSIE FELT THE days speeding up as the rodeo loomed closer and closer. They worked on the ranch and house at breakneck speed, as if Brock wanted everything to be absolutely perfect before he disappeared from their lives.

They continued fixing the perimeter fence and she

met another new patient, and suddenly another day was gone.

Three days left.

Another day on the fence, and then they only had two days until the rodeo.

Brock went around the house repairing every stuck window, squeaky hinge and unyielding kitchen drawer while Cassie unloaded the last few boxes scattered around the house.

One day left.

The last day they spent doing little things and discussing a plan for purchasing cattle over the next few years. Neither of them mentioned that it was their final day before the rodeo.

When the sun began to set, Brock asked, "Do you mind if I tuck the boys in and tell them their story?"

Cassie understood why and left the room, unable to watch Brock say not only good-night, but also goodbye. She was sure the twins would need her once he was done, but at the moment she wasn't sure she'd be able to keep her tears at bay, let alone comfort them.

As many times as she'd reminded herself about the number of days they had left and what would happen at the end of them, she still couldn't wrap her mind around the thought that she wouldn't be seeing Brock anymore.

After a while, Cassie felt composed enough to go check on the boys. In the dim room, Zach and Carter were sleeping peacefully. Brock was sitting in a chair in the corner watching them. Cassie couldn't see his face, but she knew he was as sad about their time ending as she was.

Brock stood and walked over to where she waited in the hall, shaking his head. "I just couldn't say goodbye to them," he told her.

Cassie felt hope rise in her chest. Was he saying what she thought he was saying?

"Is it okay if I come by the morning after the rodeo? Before I leave town I need to let them know I won't be around anymore. You know?" he said.

The hope she'd started to feel deflated into nothingness. He really was leaving.

Brock looked at her, and his eyes seemed to be asking her for something, but she didn't know what. Consolation? She didn't think she had it in her.

She nodded. "They'll be staying at Hank's parents' house in Glen Rock while I go to the rodeo—"

His eyes lit up and he smiled. "You're going to the rodeo?"

Cassie blushed a little. "I've never been to one, and I have a cowboy hat now. And, well…"

I needed to see you one more time.

I'm not ready to say goodbye.

I love you.

She let the sentence drift away. He could fill in the blank with whatever he liked.

"And you'll wait for me after? I'll be busy most of the day, but I can come find you as soon as my ride's over."

She didn't need to answer. Of course she would wait.

He seemed lighter, more relieved, but she couldn't share in those emotions. Whether they said goodbye right now or tomorrow or the day after, the end was the same. He would leave and she and the boys would need to pick up the pieces of their hearts.

"But the boys will be at their grandparents'?" he asked.

Cassie nodded. She didn't want her boys watching, getting ideas about bull riding if Brock did well. And if he didn't, well, she didn't want them to see that, either. Also, selfishly, she wanted her last little bit of time with him alone. "But we should probably be back by eight or so the next morning, if you're coming back here."

"I will," Brock said.

They stood there, silent. What else was there to say?

"I better get going," Brock said, not moving from where he stood.

"You have a big day tomorrow," Cassie added, hating the inanity as it came out of her mouth.

Then, as if by mutual agreement, they rushed into each other's arms, holding each other close, their lips pressed together as if they needed to concentrate hundreds of kisses in that one.

BROCK AWOKE THE next morning, more tired than he'd ever felt, as his alarm beeped incessantly. He'd come home only as the sun rose, when he finally convinced himself that it was time to leave Cassie's embrace.

He stayed in bed a few extra seconds, wishing it was a different day. It was fruitless, however, and he knew it. This was the day of the rodeo. It was going to be a painful day, he was absolutely sure, and that was because he had two big problems: he was out of shape for his ride, and he wasn't ready to say goodbye to Cassie and the twins. The thought of not being able to see the twins every day, in fact, was turning out to be harder to accept than he'd anticipated.

After this, he'd be off on his adventures and back on the circuit, and the boys would go back to life without him.

Well, he could still drop by and see them, be neighborly, that sort of thing. It was little consolation when he knew what he was giving up, but there was no way around it unless he wanted to leave behind everything in his life that he enjoyed doing.

Brock had planned to ask Cassie about seeing each other again, even if it was just for a day or two the next time he was in town, but he'd chickened out. He wasn't ready to hear her say no, and he knew that she would.

Brock sighed and sat up. At least he would see Cassie again that night, and Zach and Carter the next morning. If he held on to those thoughts and ignored the rest, he could make it through okay.

Brock drove to Glen Rock early to register for the bull-riding competition, and then he spent the next several hours with his uncle Joe. The old man growled about how out of shape he was, and how did Brock ever expect to make it to the NFR in Vegas in this condition?

Brock had no answer. He hadn't thought about the NFR in nearly two weeks. His mind had been occupied with other things.

Once he was limbered up a bit, stretching his back to try and prevent his old injury from flaring up on him at the wrong moment, there wasn't much to do but wait and chat with the other competitors. Jay came up to him immediately. "Brock! You haven't been much help planning the mine exploration. It's been like pulling teeth to get anything from you."

Brock shrugged. "I was busy," he said.

Every time he'd gotten a message from Jay, he either ignored it or gave a single-word response. He felt a little guilty every time Jay wrote, as if he was sneaking behind Cassie's back, though he knew that didn't make much sense.

"Busy? What've you been doing?" Jay asked.

Brock paused, not sure what to say. "I've been helping a neighbor," he responded finally.

Jay raised his eyebrows and smiled in a way Brock didn't care for. "*Oh.* I guess I should've asked *who* you've been doing."

"Watch it, Jay," Brock said, his jaw clenching.

All of the guys ribbed each other about their buckle bunnies, but Brock wasn't about to let that go on about Cassie.

Jay's expression didn't change one bit. "Is that why your uncle is so pissed at you? Were you so 'busy' screwing—"

For all his bulk, Brock was not a violent guy, which was why he was as surprised as anybody when his fist collided with Jay's jaw.

Brock stood there dumbfounded, not believing what he'd done, as Jay sat up from where he'd landed on the floor, rubbing at the place where Brock had hit him. The other cowboys closed in, and Brock knew that they were preparing to separate them if either one threw another punch.

"Sorry about that," he told Jay, holding out his hand.

Jay looked at the proffered hand for a second, and Brock thought he might have lost a good friend, but then Jay just laughed, took the hand and pulled himself to his feet. "Okay," he said good-humoredly. "Point taken. No more comments about the neighbor."

Jay moved on to the topic of the mines, and Brock half listened. What had gotten into him? Sure, he never participated in that particular type of talk—his ma had raised him to always speak respectfully of women—but he'd never gotten so wound up about it before.

Of course, it had never been about Cassie.

Brock ran his fingers through his hair and stood up. "I need to go find Uncle Joe," he said, more for a reason to leave than anything else.

Jay nodded, though he still looked a little confused about Brock's behavior. Brock found it hard to care too much at that moment. All he wanted to do was go look out in the stands and see if he could find a certain woman with curly brown hair underneath a white cowboy hat.

Brock found a good spot where he could see all of the stands, but before he could scan much of the crowd, Uncle Joe walked up to him, scowling. Brock couldn't believe his uncle was still that upset about his lack of preparation, but his uncle cleared things up immediately. "I just got the lineup," Brock's uncle told him. "You're tangling with Freckles today."

Brock couldn't help but laugh. Of course he would be riding Freckles with Cassie watching. He gave up any hope of doing well in front of her. He'd settle for surviving the encounter.

Brock took a deep breath and looked at the audience again, sweeping his eyes across for the wild, curly hair, the face he'd grown to know so well.

There. She'd made it. And she *was* wearing her hat, just like she said.

He wasn't sure if he was glad she was there or not, now. But just seeing her bolstered his spirits. She was even more beautiful than she'd been the night before. He soaked in the sight of her, wishing he could go to her.

As soon as he was done with his ride, he vowed, he would go into the stands. Hug her. Tell her he didn't want this thing between them to end. Not yet.

Brock's uncle started talking to him again, and Brock turned his attention back to the old rodeo pro, trying to keep his mind on the coming ride. He knew he would need all the help he could get if he was going to survive this thing.

CASSIE SAT IN the stands, waiting for Brock's turn. Each cowboy's ride filled her with more and more worry. Some seemed so close to danger, a split second from being trampled. She thought of Brock's bedtime story and wondered if there was more truth to it than she'd originally thought. Her heart stuck in her throat.

"Brock McNeal riding Freckles," a voice announced over the loudspeaker.

Cassie almost laughed when she heard the name of her silly dog, but then she remembered what Brock had told the boys about Freckles, and her worries increased tenfold. He had said he was happy he'd never ridden Freckles, that the animal was crazy.

The buzz of conversation around her didn't help, either. "Last time I saw Freckles, he 'bout killed the cowboy riding him," said a lady sitting near her.

"I hope for Brock's sake he can manage to hold on," muttered a man in a large cowboy hat.

Cassie crossed her arms, hugging herself to keep the fear at bay.

The buzzer sounded and the chute opened, and there was Brock on top of a mean-looking bull. Whoever named him must've had a terrible sense of humor, Cassie thought.

Each second went by with incredible slowness.

One, two…

Brock was holding on, moving well with the bull, and Cassie's spirits lifted.

Three, four, five…

She was watching so intently she could see the exact moment when something went wrong. Suddenly Brock was out of sync with the bull, and Cassie wanted to close her eyes, but she couldn't look away.

Six…

Brock's head slammed into Freckles's back and he slid off, lifeless. As he fell, bullfighters rushed into the arena, trying to pull the bull away from where Brock lay.

Then Freckles was gone and it was just Brock on the ground, not moving.

Cassie stared, unable to comprehend what had just happened.

Chapter Fourteen

Brock woke up slowly. He felt as if he was swimming up through an ocean of black. When he finally broke the surface and opened his eyes, he closed them again immediately to shut out the light of early morning sunshine. He didn't remember anything of the bull ride or the time that had passed since. His head pounded.

"What happened?" he asked the room, though he wasn't even sure if anyone was there with him.

"You hit your head on the bull's back and got a concussion," a voice answered.

It was Cassie. Just hearing her voice soothed him, and his head seemed to hurt less. He opened his eyes a little so he could see her. She was sitting beside his bed in what had to be a hospital room. Her cheeks were pale, but she still looked incredibly beautiful.

When their eyes met, she asked, "Who was the first president of the United States?"

Brock had gotten a couple of concussions in his life, so he knew why she asked. "George Washington. Was I pretty bad?"

"You were out of it for quite a while, but you seem to be better," Cassie said, looking into each of his eyes carefully. Brock felt lucky to be dating a doctor. "You should be up and about in time for your trip to the mines this afternoon."

Brock felt a rush of dread. How did she know about that?

"Your cowboy friends came by to check on you last night," Cassie said, responding to his unasked question.

Brock waited for her to tell him it was a stupid, dangerous idea. He almost welcomed it. Anything would be better than this sad, quiet calmness that he couldn't interpret.

Cassie stood up and slipped her purse over her shoulder. "Your family is waiting outside to see you. The last two weeks have been amazing, Brock. You've helped me more than you know. But I think it's best if things end now, for good. I'll tell Zach and Carter you said goodbye."

Brock finally got his tongue unstuck. "Goodbye?" he asked.

This couldn't be it for them, could it? Cassie shrugged. "We've always said it wasn't a permanent thing, Brock. Now that I'm sure you'll be okay, it's time for me to go."

"I don't want it to be over," he said. "I could visit—"

Cassie shook her head. "We shouldn't see each other anymore. Jay and I chatted for quite a while, and it's clear that my boys and I don't fit into your life. I'd always known that, but I can't lie to myself about it anymore. Zach and Carter need someone stable, who'll be there for them. I can't put them through another father's death. And I love you too much to watch you try to kill yourself."

She wiped away a single tear, the only sign of emotion from her.

He couldn't think what to say. His brain seemed jumbled, unable to organize his thoughts into coherent sentences. He wasn't sure if it was from the concussion or the fact that Cassie was leaving for good.

She turned away from him and walked to the door. Once there, she hesitated, and he felt hope rise in him. But then she was gone, the door shutting slowly behind her.

CASSIE LEFT THE hospital as quickly as she could, only stopping for a brief moment to say goodbye to her neighbors, Brock's parents. Once she was in the privacy of her car, she let her sobs take over. It had taken all her strength to keep herself calm while he had babbled nonsense due to the concussion, while Jay explained to her about their mine exploration plan and their past adventures, and then finally while speaking to Brock. Now, however, she could allow all the worry and sadness to wash over her.

After her tears had lessened enough so she could see, Cassie buckled her seat belt and started up her car. She made the quiet drive to pick up Zach and Carter, her mind constantly running in circles, though always with the same conclusion.

She couldn't be with Brock. She'd known it from the beginning, and the information about the mines and the other daredevil stunts he and his friends participated in was just a reminder of that fact.

As soon as she saw Zach and Carter, she pulled them into a tight hug. If nothing else, she had them. They would always be enough. "I missed you boys," she said into Carter's hair.

"Did Brock ride a bull?" Zach asked.

"He did," Cassie said, dancing a fine line between telling the truth and protecting her children. "Let's go home." She settled them into the SUV.

"Is Brock going to come tell us about riding the bull? I want to hear it as a bedtime story," Carter explained.

Cassie's heart went out to her two boys. "Actually, Brock won't be able to come by anymore. Remember when we talked about how he would be leaving Spring Valley for his job? Well," she said, trying to hold back the tears that threatened, "he won't be coming over anymore. He wanted me to say goodbye to you for him."

The looks on the boys' faces were almost more than she could bear. They looked devastated. "He's not going to tell us about the rodeo?" Zach asked.

"Can we go with him?" Carter asked.

Cassie put her head in her hands, wishing this were easier, then began to drive, hoping she would come up with something to make the pain her children were feeling hurt less.

BROCK WATCHED AS his friends put on lamp helmets and climbing gear, but he didn't make a move toward the pile of equipment. He just couldn't get himself excited about exploring the mines, even though his buddies all seemed energized and ready to go.

Brock walked toward the mine entrance and peered into the darkness, but his mind wandered to a mass of curly brown hair and green eyes, and to two matched grinning faces. He understood why Cassie had asked him to keep his distance—he didn't want to hurt the boys any more than she did, and as long as he was doing stuff like climbing into mines, that was all too real a possibility.

Brock pulled at his phone and looked at the screen, even though he knew he had no messages. Who would have sent him one?

The phone buzzed in his hand, and he had a moment of hope before he saw that he'd received a text from Ma. Cassie might be moving away. I saw her packing. Thought you'd want to know.

The blood drained out of Brock's face as he absorbed the words. She was packing?

Then he realized what that meant. If he didn't do something quickly, he was going to lose her for good.

Brock looked toward his friends, who were geared up and ready to walk into the dark, abandoned entrance and he knew what he had to do. There was someplace he needed to be, and it had nothing to do with mines.

"Where are you going?" Jay asked, but Brock didn't have time to answer. As he opened his truck door, Jay called out, "Is it the neighbor?"

"I'll let you know how it goes!" Brock shouted back.

He heard Jay yell, "Good luck!" as he started down the dirt road that would lead him to the highway and Spring Valley.

BROCK PARKED IN front of Cassie's house and hopped out of his truck. He hardly had a chance to wonder why the front door was open as he bolted through it and to Cassie's office, where she was standing with an older woman he recognized from town. Probably a patient.

Neither noticed him.

Cassie and the woman hugged, and Cassie said, "I'll miss you, Mrs. Edelman."

His heart tightened painfully. "Please don't leave Spring Valley," he said, knowing he was begging but unable to care.

The older woman glared at him. "I will so leave Spring Valley, young man, and no green rascal is going to stop me," she said, pointing her finger at him.

Brock was confused, but he couldn't deal with that right now. There was too much at risk to lose focus. He rushed up to Cassie and gave her a kiss. He couldn't help himself. She seemed at a loss for words, but the way her body molded to his gave him hope. "I don't want to lose you and the boys, Cassie. I love you. All three of you. I'd rather be a husband and a father than a lonely thrill-seeker." He rubbed his thumb along her bottom lip, memorizing its shape. "Please don't go back to Minneapolis. I can't say goodbye to you."

Her expression went through several changes, from surprise to what he hoped was love, then to confusion. "Who told you I was leaving?"

"Ma saw you packing. The moment I thought I might never see you again, I knew I wanted to be with you forever. You and Zach and Carter give me something to live for."

This time, she initiated the kiss, and he wrapped his arms around her. For a long moment, they stood entwined.

Then the patter of tiny feet heralded the entrance of the twins, who shouted Brock's name in excitement. Brock knelt to the floor and accepted their hugs. He didn't think he'd ever felt happier than at that moment.

His ma poked her head into the room. "I'll be taking the boys now, Cassie. We'll be back in a couple of hours, after I've spoiled them properly." She turned to Brock, a satisfied smile on her face. "Came to your senses, did you?"

"Why did you tell Brock I was leaving?" Cassie asked the older woman.

"Technically, I said I saw you packing, dear. Which was true—you packed toys into these backpacks," Sarah explained, pointing at the backpacks the twins were wearing. "And it wasn't all my idea."

"Did it work?" Emmaline Reynolds asked, coming in from the other room.

"Emma?" Cassie asked her friend.

Emma shrugged, and Brock's ma smirked. "I knew he'd figure things out eventually, but it seemed best to light a fire under him. Now the boys and I will get out of your hair."

"And I'll take Mrs. Edelman home. She leaves for her big trip tomorrow, you know. Sorry again about

Danny canceling his appointment, but I assume you can find some way to fill the time," Emma said, giving her friend a wink before walking out.

The hall cleared out as quickly as it had filled, and Brock turned to Cassie, who was shaking her head and laughing. It took him a moment to fully register what had happened. "You were never planning to leave," he said. It wasn't a question.

Cassie shook her head. "Want to take back anything you said now that you know I'm not giving up on my dream because of you?"

He moved close to her, reveling in her vanilla scent. "Not one bit," he said, happy.

"I thought you loved your thrill-seeking life," she said.

"Funny thing," he said thoughtfully. "I always thought that if I had kids, I would need to give up everything I enjoy because I didn't want them to grow up without a father.

"But I had it backward," he continued. "I don't want to do dangerous things anymore because I don't want to miss a single minute of them growing up. Risking your life doesn't seem as much fun when you have that at stake."

They heard the front door close, and silence surrounded them, Brock realized they were alone. Cassie seemed to notice the same thing. "I have another patient coming later today," she said.

Brock brushed the hair out of her face. "Would you be able to make a little time for me first, Doc? I've had a recent head injury."

Cassie knitted her eyebrows. "That's right. How are you feeling?" she asked as she placed her palm against his cheek and looked in his eyes.

Brock smiled. "Better than ever," he said, leaning down for another kiss.

* * * * *

*If you loved this novel,
don't miss the next book in Ali Olson's*
SPRING VALLEY, TEXAS *series
coming in April 2018
from Harlequin Western Romance!*

COMING NEXT MONTH FROM

HARLEQUIN®

Western Romance

Available February 6, 2018

#1677 THE COWBOY'S TEXAS TWINS
Cupid's Bow, Texas • by Tanya Michaels
Becoming guardian to his twin godsons has thrown rodeo cowboy Grayson harder than any bronc! But falling for town librarian Hadley Lanier just might heal his bruised heart.

#1678 HER COWBOY REUNION
Made in Montana • by Debbi Rawlins
No one recognizes the savvy businesswoman Savannah James has become when she returns to Blackfoot Falls. Except her former neighbor, Mike Burnett, who is willing to keep her secret...but can't resist rekindling an old attraction!

#1679 RODEO SHERIFF
Rodeo, Montana • by Mary Sullivan
Sheriff Cole Payette has always loved Honey Armstrong, not that she's noticed. And when he's charged with raising his sister's children, Honey's the only one he can trust with the kids—and his heart.

#1680 A FAMILY FOR THE RANCHER
Cowboys to Grooms • by Allison B. Collins
Nash Sullivan, a combat vet with a missing leg, survivor's guilt and a scarred heart, is determined to keep everyone at a distance. His new physical therapist, single mom Kelsey Summers, has other plans!

YOU CAN FIND MORE INFORMATION ON UPCOMING HARLEQUIN® TITLES, FREE EXCERPTS AND MORE AT WWW.HARLEQUIN.COM.

HWESTCNM0118

Get 2 Free Books,
Plus 2 Free Gifts—
just for trying the Reader Service!

HARLEQUIN®
Western Romance

HWRI7R2

As Hadley made her way toward the back of the store, a crash reverberated.

She heard a man's voice, followed by a high-pitched wail. Then a little boy yelled, "You made my brother cry!"

"Sam, I didn't— Tyler, don't… Boys, please!"

Momentarily abandoning her cart, Hadley peeked around the corner at the cereal aisle.

Boxes were everywhere. Among the cardboard wreckage, one boy sobbed facedown on the floor while another sat a few feet away, his eyes suspiciously dry. It took her a second to realize the boys were identical.

She cleared her throat. "Need a hand?"

The man whipped his head around. "Sorry about the disturbance, ma'am."

Flashing him a reassuring smile, she kneeled to retrieve a dented cereal box. "This hardly qualifies as a disturbance. You should see the library on story day when half the audience needs a nap."

He gave her a grin, and dimples appeared. *Oh, mercy!*

"What the heck happened here?"

Hadley glanced past Dimples to find a bewildered Violet Duncan.

The horizontal twin lifted his tearstained face. "It w-w-was a accident!"

"Grayson yelled at Sam!" the other twin accused.

Grayson…

Good Lord. Dimples was Grayson Cox? Hadley hadn't recognized her former classmate.

"I did not yell!" Grayson defended himself. "I told him to stop running, which he didn't, and then I pointed out the consequences of not listening."

Violet scooped up Sam and set him in the shopping cart. The action startled the boy out of his crying.

"If you and your brother will behave, you can come help me pick out something for dessert tonight." With a sigh, Violet turned to Grayson. "You want to finish restoring order here and meet us in the baking aisle?"

"Yes, ma'am." He ducked his gaze, looking as boyishly chagrined as young Sam.

When Hadley chuckled at his expression, all eyes turned to her.

Violet gave her a smile. "Hey, Hadley."

"Hadley?" Grayson echoed, turning back toward her. He blinked. "Hadley Lanier?"

She couldn't believe she hadn't recognized him sooner— or that she had yet to look away. *Quit staring.* Easier said than done. "I, uh… What was the question? Oh!" Her cheeks burned. "Yes. I'm Hadley."

Don't miss THE COWBOY'S TEXAS TWINS
by Tanya Michaels, available February 2018
wherever Harlequin® Western Romance books
and ebooks are sold.

www.Harlequin.com

HWREXP0118

Looking for more satisfying love stories
with community and family at their core?

Check out **Harlequin® Special Edition**
and **Harlequin® Western Romance** books!

New books available every month!

CONNECT WITH US AT:

Harlequin.com/Community

ReaderService.com

**ROMANCE WHEN
YOU NEED IT**

HFGENRE2017R

Reward the book lover in you!

Earn points from all your Harlequin book purchases from wherever you shop.

Turn your points into *FREE BOOKS* of your choice
OR
EXCLUSIVE GIFTS from your favorite authors or series.

Join for FREE today at
www.HarlequinMyRewards.com.

Harlequin My Rewards is a free program (no fees) without any commitments or obligations.

MYR17